Jackson's Song

Rachel Lopez

rachelrlopez.com

Jackson's Song
Copyright © 2021 by Rachel Lopez.

For information contact:
Synecdoche Publishing
synecdochepublishing.wordpress.com

Edited by Emily Burkey and Amanda Hovseth
Book design by Amanda Hovseth
Cover by KA Designs

ISBN: 978-1-945018-21-3 (soft cover); 978-1-945018-22-0 (eBook)

Library of Congress Control Number: 2021932459

First Edition: 2021

Jackson's Song is dedicated to
Tavon Breckenridge

Tavon Desmond Breckenridge

Born 12/20/1997 - Called Home 02/12/2019

Forward

By the time you reach the end of my tale, I pray you'll be moved to make a change. That you'll be inspired to stand against the evils of this world, one bullied child at a time. Maybe you'll become kinder, more compassionate, work to stop senseless bullying, or maybe you will simply learn to love yourself. Perhaps you're like me and tormented by those around you; be patient, God will deliver you from your trials. Whatever the end result, don't let my actions have been in vain. Drink in my story, allow my words to speak to your heart for those who have moved on from this place…let me speak for those of you who haven't yet found your voice.

-Jackson

Chapter One

In darkness I find my comfort, but your bright light saw me through.
How was I to know you would be the one to break me?
How was I to know it would be you?

"Jackson, are you ready to talk?" Dr. Todd asked, her pretty brown eyes encouraging me to bare my soul.

"We've been talking," I spoke through clenched teeth. I wasn't in the mood, and she knew it. It was the same thing with her every single day. I was tired of talking. Not only was I tired of talking, claustrophobia was setting in.

My eyes scanned the tiny room—it had become my prison—the walls closed in upon me. I wanted to scream until my throat closed in upon itself. However, unprovoked screaming episodes would ensure an even longer stay at Manchester Spinal Institute. Most likely, my stay would be in a luxurious white padded room on the tenth floor where I would be awarded a form fitting white jacket.

I was used to holding my emotions in. I didn't know how to share my feelings unless they spewed out of my mouth…accidentally…in a volcanic fit of rage. Deep down, I knew I needed to talk to Dr. Todd. But with me being an awkward teen boy, and her a beautiful woman—it was hard to be vulnerable in front of her.

The last few days, Dr. Todd had pressed me to share my story. Today was the closest she had gotten to opening me up, but once again I backed out. It would only be a matter of time before she'd get me to crack. The good thing about Dr. Todd: she was gently relentless, especially when it came to matters of the soul. Unfortunately for me, I was the one she was being relentless with. The look of wild determination in her eyes had begun to wear me down. I was fighting a losing battle.

"Yes, Jackson, but I need you to talk to me about—that day at school if you want to make any progress." Her words were tinged with desperation. "You do want me to sign off on your discharge paperwork to get you out of here, don't you?"

She waved her arm in the air indicating my hobbit hole. It wasn't a rhetorical question. She wanted an answer, but at this point I didn't have one. I looked at her pointedly until her eyes broke away.

Dr. Todd let out a small sigh and shook her head in defeat. "Okay, well if you're not going to tell me about that day then we need to talk about something else. How was school life before then?"

My mind sifted through my life—the good, the bad, and the ugly. For several seconds I thought about the day that had started it all. I suppose there would be no harm in sharing—a little—with her.

"Okay..." I said, taking in a big deep breath, allowing it to flow through my mouth as loudly as possible. I believe there may have been an eye roll involved as well. "I guess I should start with my first day of middle school. That's when…things changed."

A fresh rush of shame washed over me; my face grew hot thinking back to that day. Talking about the past wasn't a good idea, but I had given Dr. Todd a hard time earlier, and I didn't think she would take much more from me.

Actually, I was already in trouble with my mother for poor behavior with the nurses, so I figured I better cooperate. Another bad report and I was toast. To be honest, even though I was giving Dr. Todd a hard time, she was one of the few people I trusted, and I did enjoy talking to her most of the time.

"It was the first day of sixth grade, and I was nervous about switching to a bigger school, but I was excited to see my friends after a long summer away."

The words left my mouth, but I was no longer with Dr. Todd. I was walking through the hallways of Melon Croft Middle School. Laughter filled every corner of the freshly painted building. The sweet scent of cinnamon rolls invaded my nostrils. It was good to be back at school, yet a twinge of nervousness tightened up inside of me.

"The floors were shiny, I remember looking down, and seeing my distorted reflection in them, my face a wavy bulbous melon. The scent of wax and new school supplies almost overpowered the cinnamon rolls, but not quite. There's a distinct smell to the first day of school, you know?" I looked at Dr. Todd to see if she thought what I said was odd, but she gave me a knowing smile and nodded for me to continue.

"My first class was packed by the time I arrived, so I picked an empty seat in the middle of the room and readied myself for the start of class. I enjoyed the first day of school; I loved pulling out my new supplies and arranging them carefully on my desk. Everything was so new—the classes, the people, everything—but that was just part of the excitement for me. I loved meeting new people—making new friends."

"Each class went as well as my first, which was great, and I felt middle school was going to be amazing." An ironic chuckle left my lips. "I was thinking how silly I had been for all the anxiety and worry I had felt about switching to a bigger school, when I ran into my nightmare—literally, ran right into him." I paused, reliving that moment. My throat grew tight and my face burned with embarrassment, but I continued.

"It was time for lunch, and I was in a hurry to get to the cafeteria. I was starving. It felt like days had gone by since breakfast. I remember I...I grabbed my lunch bag out of my locker, then I shot back into the hallway. I wasn't paying attention, and the next thing I knew, bam, I ran into Brett Watters. He was caught off guard and fell to the ground; his books and papers flew from his hands scattering across the hallway."

"Before I realized what happened, Brett jumped back to his feet, grabbed me by my throat, and slammed me into the lockers." Hot tears streamed down my face. I remembered the humiliation of Brett running my body up those lockers, my feet dangling in the air.

"Desperately, I fought to pry his fingers from my throat, but he was stronger than I was. 'Who do you think you are, kid? Huh?'" With a shaky voice, I repeated the words that seared themselves into my memory. I had nightmares of those words. "Brett's dark bloodshot eyes zeroed in on mine, his face blood red. Apparently, I'd made him appear...foolish?" I paused and shrugged like it wasn't a big deal, but Dr. Todd and I clearly knew better.

"His breath was hot against my face, and I tried not to look at him. I thought maybe if I didn't look directly into his eyes, then he would leave me alone," I added lamely. In reality, I was scared out of my wits, and didn't know what to do. I was lucky I hadn't wet myself.

"'I'm...I'm sorry,' I choked out an apology, but his grip was tight and I was terrified. I've never encountered someone so completely..." I trailed off for a moment, at a loss for words when it came to describing Brett...I continued my story. "Brett finally let me go, and I crumpled to the ground. I curled into a ball and hid my face until he was done with me."

I wish I had never shown him how weak I was that day. I had beaten myself up about that incident hundreds of times. Maybe things wouldn't have been so bad, had I stood up for myself. But we can't live in "what ifs" or we would drive ourselves crazy, or at least that's what my mom says.

"Before he left," I went on, "Brett bent over and whispered in my ear, 'I'm going to make you wish you were never born,' and he did—many times over."

As I finished my story I looked at Dr. Todd to study her reaction. I despised the pity reflecting in her eyes.

Dr. Todd sensed what I was feeling, but threw more questions my way. "Was Brett the only person who bullied you?" she asked, scrawling away in her notebook.

"No, he started it, and he was always the worst offender, but I lost all of my friends… they were afraid of being treated the same way," I answered. Now I was definitely feeling sorry for myself, which wasn't a good thing. Feeling sorry for myself is what landed me in my current situation. "You know," I said with a laugh. "I thought this year was going to be good for me. Brett was supposed to move on to high school, and that would've given me a Brett free year, but he failed the eighth grade. So instead of a year without humiliation and pain, it came at me twofold. The more he picked on me the braver the other kids became." I had always thought when we got older my peers would mature and the bullying would go away, but time only seemed to make it worse.

"How many kids bullied you, Jackson?" she asked. She was speaking gently now, careful to not damage my fragile mind.

"Too many to count." My eyes teared up again. I hoped Dr. Todd would leave soon. There was nothing I hated more than for someone to see me cry. Dr. Todd was one of the few people I allowed to see the real me, the raw damaged shell of a…what was I?

"How often did the bullying happen?" That's how Dr. Todd was; she pushed question after question on me, each one worse than the one before. As maddening as her methods appeared, they worked on me, I always shared more than I intended. One of the nurses told me they would hate to see Dr. Todd as a patient, because she makes them think too much. The nurse wasn't wrong, but I suppose in my case I needed to explore the dark corners of my mind.

"Every day," I whispered, mentally shutting down.

"Just a few more minutes, Jackson, we will be done soon." She was truly upset for me, but at this point nothing could be done.

"Can you give me some examples of what the bullies did to you?" she asked.

Maybe it was the endless barrage of questions, the hard day of therapy, or maybe it was her innocence that pushed me to my limit, but I decided to shock her a bit. Maybe she would leave me alone if I shared my "war wounds" with her, revealed my pain. In my anguish, I wanted to punish her for what she didn't understand. She needed to see why it was hard for me to talk about what I had gone through.

"See this?" I pointed to a dark, round scar on my upper arm. "This is where a kid stabbed me with an ink pen. Mom had to take me to the emergency room, and I received three stitches. I told her I was running with a pen in my hand and fell." Dr. Todd's mouth hung open, stunned, but I plowed on with my show and tell.

"Let's see." I studied my body trying to make a production of my 'show and tell'. "Oh yes, here." I held up my left hand revealing two very crooked fingers.

"This is where Jacob Michaels broke my fingers. I sat next to him in science class and he didn't want me near him. He just grabbed them like this," I gathered my fingers with my other hand and wrenched them to the side. "Mom never knew about that one. I suffered until they healed on their own; it took months. Oh and here," indicating a long grayish mark on my forearm. "This is where Brett slammed my arm shut in my locker. That didn't need stitches, but it hurt pretty bad."

I was planning to further enlighten Dr. Todd, but she held her hand up to silence me. She closed her eyes, and twisted her face in disgust. If truth be told, her golden skin turned a bit greenish.

"Okay, I get it. Jackson, are you telling me these kids bullied and physically harmed you for years and no one attempted to help you?"

Dr. Todd's voice rose a few octaves, and had become rather screechy. I shrugged my shoulders. For me, that was how life had been. Dr. Todd was naive about how teenagers worked. I thought this kind of behavior was pretty common, but maybe I had become a product of my surroundings, I don't know.

"Who would help me?" I asked, my voice rising, a direct match to Dr. Todd's. She wanted me to admit I had options, that I had the power to stop the torture. She wanted me to see there were people who would help me in my time of need. She was wrong.

Her jaw opened and shut a few times unsure of what to say. "Friends, family, teachers, the principal?" she shot back. Her flawless cheeks turned a nice shade of pink—she was upset–not at me but at how crappy my situation really was.

Dr. Todd must have been one of those sheltered kids who never dealt with bullying a day in her life. Looking at her, I couldn't imagine anyone not liking her. She looked like one of those all-American cheerleading types turned super professional, businesslike. Like a tall blond-haired blue-eyed Barbie someone had slapped a pair of black plastic Clark Kent eye frames on.

"All the teachers ducked their heads and looked the other way. They didn't want to deal with Brett any more than I did. And as for friends, I have none and I haven't for years. They abandoned me when the bullying started. I tried telling once, and the next time Brett got his hands on me I received this." Pulling the sheets back, I show her another large scar on my right knee from a nasty "fall" I had taken.

"There was one person who I thought was a friend, but in the end she was like everyone else." I wasn't going to talk about that person—not yet. My heart still broke when I thought about how little I meant to her. If I meant anything at all, she would've been by my side. One day, people would realize how important it is to stand up for those who can't stand up for themselves; I was going to make sure of it.

"What about your mother?" Dr. Todd asked. She put her pen down. This was something she wanted to know for herself. By her disapproving tone and tight lips, I could tell she didn't think highly of my mother's lack of knowledge when it came to what was going on in her son's life.

"It's not her fault. When kids like me want to hide things…like this…we're good at it. Mom didn't know much. There were a few instances when she stepped in, but for the most part she had no idea." My teenage pride prevented me from showing my mom what a failure I was. "When dad left…I felt…like I was supposed to be the man of the house, you know? Anyway, I brushed the abuse off with excuses like, 'Oh Mom, me and the guys were goofing around,' or, 'I fell playing ball with my buddies,' or, 'it was an accident.'" I rattled off a few of my frequently used excuses.

"I tried to keep it away from my mother. If I was going to cry, I did it in the school bathroom or I would hold it in until everyone was asleep at night. Sometimes I let it out when I played guitar so she couldn't hear me." I shrugged.

"You play guitar?" she asked, perking up.

"Yeah, it's the one thing I'm kinda decent at," I shrugged, feeling my face go red.

"What kind of music do you play?

"Uh some rock, but lately I've been writing my own music. I mean, I was until…until I came here."

Dr. Todd watched me for a minute. "Yeah, I can see it."

Confused I cocked my head, "See what?"

"You, being a rock star."

"Nah, not now," I looked down at my legs.

"Yes, especially now, Jackson. You should ask your mom to bring your guitar up here, I would love to hear you play."

"I dunno, I'll think about it." For once she let it go and said no more about me bringing my guitar.

"So, your doctor has recommended you to come down to my office for appointments from now on if that is okay with you?" Dr. Todd didn't look up at me but wrote some notes in on her tablet.

"Uh, sure that's fine, I guess I need to get out of here a little more."

Nervously, Dr. Todd smiled at my answer. "That's great. How about tomorrow before physical therapy? I am in room 510. It's on the fifth floor right off of elevator B. Here, I'll leave you a card with the number on it. If therapy runs late just have them call my extension."

"Cool, thanks." I answered, taking the card from her outstretched hand.

After that, Dr. Todd decided to call it a day, and I completely agreed. Finally, I had bared my soul, somewhat, and I felt oddly relieved. The shame I felt on a day-to-day basis was significantly less than it had been after my talk with Dr. Todd—except, there was so much more waiting to break free. The only way to be rid of the burden was to share what caused me to finally break. However, it was too difficult to say it out loud. So I decided to do the only thing I could do, and write down what happened to me that terrible spring day. The day my life changed forever.

Chapter Two

Eight Months Earlier

"Jackson, time to get up, love," my mother sang through my door. She's one of those chipper morning people. Some mornings her peppiness drove me insane, but not that morning. That particular morning I woke up in a wonderful mood. It was the day my life was going to change; I would no longer be ruled by fear.

"I'm awake," I shouted while rubbing the sleep from my eyes. I stumbled over to my closet.

"Wake your sister before you come down," she said, retreating downstairs to cook breakfast.

"Okay…" I half spoke, half yawned. Slightly distracted, I tried to decide which shirt to wear. It was a toss-up between my Marvel comic t-shirt and my light blue polo. My Marvel tee won; it was my lucky shirt. Besides, the blue polo had a small ketchup stain on the collar. I needed to look nice.

As soon as I was dressed, I went to the bathroom that separates Lilly's room and mine. I was relieved to see the bathroom open. If Lilly got up before I did (which was rare), she tied up the restroom until it was time to leave for school.

Looking at myself in the mirror, I liked what I saw—for the first time in a long time I was able to see a normal kid and not the school freak. I was a pretty average looking guy. My dark brown eyes were a replica of my mother's, but my large nose, dark brown hair, and long lanky frame came from my father. At that moment, I had a pretty decent tan from helping mom with the garden. It felt good to see I was outgrowing the awkwardness that plagued me my entire middle school career.

"Hey, how's it going," I said, raising my eyebrows at my reflection. "Oh yeah? Me too…" I said, flexing my nonexistent bicep in the mirror.

"Jackson," my mother said, rapping sharply on the door. Like a grasshopper, I jumped a foot in the air, knocking the toothbrush holder off the sink and straight into the toilet. As was typical with my luck, only my toothbrush floated in the blue liquid filled bowl.

"Dang it, mom!"

"Who are you talking to?" she asked.

"No one. I was…just singing…" I answered distractedly, fishing my toothbrush out. Thankfully I had flushed.

"Well, hurry up. I'm volunteering at the hospital this morning and don't want to be late."

"Got it." Once again I heard Mom's feet retreating. Moments later, after scalding my toothbrush, I stepped into the hallway and opened the door to Lilly's room.

The door squeaked. I stopped in my tracks as she rustled under her comforter from the noise. She settled back down and snuggled her face in her lace-lined pillow. My sister looked so innocent—her life was simple. This may sound weird, but I've got to say, I really love my kid sister.

Lilly just turned seven, and she looked like a mini sleeping beauty. She was small and graceful with strawberry blonde hair that curled loosely around her dainty face. Her enormous brown eyes were like my own. When she talked, she sounded like a tree elf which made her more adorable. Everyone loved Lilly from the moment they met her.

"Hey, Lil, wake up, it's time for school," I said softly, walking over to her bed. Immediately, her eyes popped open and she yawned really big. For a few minutes she lay there blinking her eyes against the hallway light that shone into her room.

Once her over-exaggerated yawn was completed, she looked at me, and said, "I love you, Jax," while trying, unsuccessfully, to stifle another yawn. See what I mean? Cute.

"I love you too. Now get up and get ready so we're not late this morning. Mom has to get to the hospital." I ruffled the wild mane on her head, and she squalled as she wiggled away from me.

Before heading downstairs, I ran to my room and grabbed my book bag. Then I flew downstairs, two at a time, to see what Mom had made for breakfast. The smell of bacon hit my nose before my foot touched the bottom stair. Immediately, my mouth began to water, and my stomach growled. There's nothing like the smell of bacon cooking in the morning, nothing. In the kitchen, I could see Mom was hard at work mixing a batch of blueberry pancakes, another one of my favorites.

While Mom finished cooking, I set the table and poured drinks for Lilly and myself. Then I dug into the giant stack of pancakes already on the table and didn't stop shoveling food into my mouth until I couldn't physically force any more into my body.

"Hey Jax, I'm going to run outside and check on the roses. It got pretty cold last night and I forgot to cover them."

"Okay, do you need help?"

"No, just make sure Lilly eats."

"Sure," I said, getting up to rinse off my plate.

I wanted to help in the garden, but I wouldn't have time this morning once I cleaned up the breakfast mess. It was a deal Lilly and I made with Mom: she cooked us a nice breakfast on school days, and we pulled clean-up duty. But working in the garden with my mother was something that relaxed me. Most of the time, I brought my guitar out and sang to the flowers and mom. I had read in a magazine once that plants loved music. There was something peaceful in escaping life for a little bit. A piece of paradise resided in my backyard in the form of my mother's garden.

When I got older, I wanted to be a botanist if my singing career fell through. Who knows, maybe I could be a singing botanist. My love for plants and flowers was a little strange for a boy my age, but it wasn't just flowers and roses.

There's so much to learn about plants, trees, and fungi. Mom and I planned to start our own greenhouse that summer once school was out. It would be mostly mine to experiment with new plants and flowers, but eventually I would like to open a mini nursery. All of which won me absolutely no points with the kids at school when I shared my 'What I want to be when I grow up' term paper the first week of sixth grade.

"Jackson, I'm hungry," Lilly's tiny voice said.

"Well, well mademoiselle, have a seat and for you I will prepare a treat," I said in a terrible French accent while draping a highly stained dish towel across my forearm. If truth be told, I sounded like I came from the Deep South.

Lilly giggled, climbed onto her chair, and waited for me to serve her breakfast. She was a bit spoiled, but I didn't mind helping mom take care of her. Sometimes, I felt like I needed to care for and protect her since dad was no longer around.

"Ahh oui oui mon cheri, eat your food so we can leave." Another giggle, but then Lilly got down to business. I mean, I can put some food away, but Lilly's butterfly frame could give me a run for my money in a pancake eating contest.

Luckily for me, Lilly finished eating quickly, and we were able to leave on time. "Oh, shoot! I forgot my…history notebook." I ran back into the house before mom could remind me I didn't take history.

Grabbing a pair of kitchen shears from the butcher's block on the counter, I bolted out the back door. Carefully I choose six of the daintiest pink roses from Mom's garden and clipped them. I wrapped a damp paper towel around the stems. Then I placed them carefully in my book bag, so no one would notice.

"Um, you ready?" Mom asked.

"Yup," I said.

"You know you don't take history, right?" Mom asked, her eyes burning into the side of my head.

"Yup," I replied my face growing hot.

"Do I need to ask if you are up to something?" The lasers from her eyes were penetrating my brain.

"Nope," I replied. *Stay strong Jackson.*

Mom studied me for a moment, then threw the car into reverse. She must have decided either that I was trustworthy, or that she would rather not know what I was up to. Thankful for a non-nosey mother, I kept my eyes trained forward the entire way to school.

Located about two miles from our house, Lilly's school and my school were right next to each other. We usually made it there in no time, and this morning was no exception. However, I was excited to get to school that day and the drive seemed to last an hour. My leg jumped up and down a million miles a second. It was shaking so hard our second-hand Toyota vibrated.

"What's up, jack rabbit? You seem wound up today," Mom asked.

I tried to play it cool. "Just eager to get to school." Her disbelief filled the car. She opened her mouth to ask once again if I were up to something. However, since we had pulled into the drop-off line, I jumped out of the car and shut the door before she had a chance to question me further.

That was a pivotal moment in my life. I should've said goodbye or told her I loved her. Mom always said hindsight was 20/20, but I never really understood what that meant until I looked back on the mistakes I made that day. *I'm so sorry mom.*

However, right then I wasn't thinking of my mother or anyone else—only Brittney Wagner. Brittney was my science project partner, and I was secretly in love with her. For the last few weeks, Brittney and I had been working on a project together. By the way she laughed at my jokes and smiled my way, I thought she might like me too. She was newer to our school and didn't yet know about the stigma associated with being my friend.

For the first time in three years, someone besides my family actually enjoyed being around me, and so far she didn't care what anyone else thought. Since we started working on our project together, my heart had been light and carefree—two emotions I hadn't felt in a long time. It didn't even faze me when Brett photoshopped a picture of my head onto an old woman's bikini clad body and shared it on social media. And by 'shared on social media' I mean every single media outlet he had access to.

As soon as my mother dropped me off, my eyes eagerly scanned the school yard looking for Brittney. We were supposed to meet that morning to talk about our project. She wasn't hanging out on the stairs where we had planned to meet, so I waited for her to show up.

I stood on the stairs, puffed out my chest, and curled my upper body outward slightly to show off my bulk. Ten seconds later, my muscles grew tired and my lanky frame slumped down in my normal, slightly hunchbacked stance. I checked my watch, hoping Brittney wouldn't be too long. I didn't want to be late for homeroom.

Really, the wait wasn't so bad. It was a lovely spring morning, and I completely zoned out everything around me except for the beauty of the day itself.

Everything about the first part of that day still vividly plays in my mind. Robins chirping, flying from one large oak to the next. The students at Melon Croft Middle School were quite fortunate actually; you couldn't ask for a more beautiful location. Large oak trees spread across the grounds, and flower beds surrounded the school in a burst of reds and white (our school colors).

In the distance, rolling hills covered by forests went on for miles surrounding the school. It was definitely a great place to enjoy nature, which I did. I guess when you have few friends in the world, you find ways to fill your time; and for me, it was being outside enjoying the scenery. As a matter of fact, a majority of my free time was spent sitting outside daydreaming. My mother was the same way. Maybe I got it from her.

After about five minutes of watching a family of blue jays build a nest, I was brought back to reality by Brittney tapping me on the shoulder. As I turned to look at her, I was rendered speechless. She was so beautiful. That day her long, honey-colored hair trailed over her shoulder in a long braid. She wore skinny jeans, tall brown riding boots, and a light green shirt that matched her eyes almost exactly. She looked as if she had stepped off the cover of one of those magazines teen girls read.

"Sorry I'm late. My mom lost her car keys this morning," she said, her green eyes shining like precious jade. Nervously, her fingers tugged at a cross necklace that encircled her neck.

"No problem," I answered. "I just got here myself."

"We better talk on the way or we'll be late," Brittney said. She hooked her arm through mine and dragged me behind her.

At her touch, my heart flipped in my chest. It had been a long time since someone besides my mother or sister had touched me. In that moment, I believed I could've exploded with happiness. Brittney was the first girl who had shown any interest in me and I was downright giddy.

There was a slight sinking feeling in the pit of my stomach. *Would she learn to hate me like everyone else?* Brittney was growing rather popular I wasn't sure she would give that up for me. She wasn't one of those snotty rich kids people liked just to fit in; she was kind and compassionate and gave everyone a chance. There wasn't a single person who didn't like her. Of course, no one really talked to me, so what did I know? One thing I knew for certain—I was her biggest fan.

So, I did what any nerdy, inexperienced kid my age would do and followed that girl like a lovesick pup. My head nodded in agreement with every word she spoke. For the most part, I had no idea what she was talking about. I had never felt this way before, but it was a wonderful feeling. With her on my arm I strutted down the school hallway with my head held high, and my chest puffed out like a rooster. I turned my head to steal a quick glance at her, but she was staring at me waiting for an answer.

"Whaaa.." I started.

"I was saying, we should meet today for lunch, maybe at The Grove," she repeated. Her eyebrows rose expectantly.

"Ah…well…sure," I answered, positively beaming. I had planned to ask her the very same question, the moment my brain began to properly function.

"The Grove" was a small cluster of great oak trees, outside the cafeteria, with picnic tables scattered underneath. It's a place for students to eat outside if they wished. Usually, the older or more popular kids got tables out there. By older and more popular kids, I mean the kids who made it their life-long goal to make me miserable.

"You know, to work on our project." The look she gave me made my knees go weak. Man, I had it bad.

No matter how heavy the rock of dread grew in the pit of my stomach, I was meeting Brittney outside to eat. Most of the kids who hung out at The Grove were cruel to me. However, I had promised myself I wouldn't allow these kids to hurt me any longer. Now was my chance to prove to myself and everyone else that I was just like them. My new-found relationship with Brittney depended on it. I had a surprise for Brittney, and I needed to do it before I could talk myself out of it.

Not wanting her to see my concern, I decided to play it cool. My attempt ended in complete disaster; however, due to the fact that my voice honked, literally like a goose.

"Thaaa," my voice squawked.

My cheeks blazed. I was mortified. Brittney was kind enough to pretend she hadn't noticed, but the pink circles that appeared along her cheeks betrayed her.

I cleared my throat and tried again. "That sounds cool, I bring my lunch so I should get outside before you do. That will give me time to set out the ros...uh, information for our project," I answered quickly, trying to cover my blunder.

"Great! I've got some sketches I want to show you," she said, pulling a few books out of her locker. "Well, I gotta go. See you at lunch."

The warm touch of her lips pressed against my cheek sent my head reeling. All I could do was stand in the hallway like a dummy, my mouth gaping. Yeah, I looked goofy but it didn't matter. As soon as she kissed me, she took off down the hall. After the initial shock wore off, I shook my head and carried myself off to my first class of the day.

The rest of that morning was agony for me. I was torn between wanting to see Brittney and being terrified to see her. What would my classmates think when they saw me sitting in The Grove—like I was one of them. My emotions were all mixed up, and I didn't know how to process them all at the same time. What I did know was that I had to have Brittney as my girl.

For three agonizing hours, I thought only of her and what I should do. At the end of that time, I felt even less sure than I did to begin with, but I knew that no matter what, by the end of the day Brittney would be my girlfriend. When the lunch bell rang, I stood from my desk, threw my shoulders back, and walked toward my future, telling myself today was my lucky day. I convinced myself nothing could go wrong.

Chapter Three

Hearing the lunch bell ring, I scrambled to get my belongings into my book bag so I could beat Brittney to "our" meeting spot. On the way, I stopped at my locker to pick up my lunch bag, the roses I picked that morning, and my guitar. For the first time, I was glad no one wanted to be my locker partner, or my guitar would've never fit. My palms grew sweaty and the words to my song, her song, floated haphazardly through my mind waiting for me to order them into submission.

"You got this, you got this, you got this," I whispered to myself.

"Gah, he's so weird," a girl two lockers down murmured. Nothing new to me. I didn't even turn my eyes her way, I just marched out the side door juggling my bookbag, lunch, and guitar all in my hands.

Just as I thought, I made it outside before she did. To save time, I took the liberty of choosing a table under the big oak trees before all the good ones were taken. We were fortunate the school allowed us to have lunch outside when it was nice. There weren't many schools who allowed their students to do that. Too much of a hassle, I suppose.

On a normal friendless day, I would've found a place on the ground far out of eyesight of my peers. There I would enjoy whatever treats my mother had packed for me. From afar I would watch the other kids laughing and goofing off; even the nerds had each other. They left me longing for a friend. But today was different. For once, I actually had someone to share my time with. Just the thought of Brittney brought a smile to my face.

While I waited for her to join me, I decided to set out the materials for our project. I set the roses to the side of the table and covered them with my science folder. I wanted them to be a surprise. On the opposite side of the large tree, I propped my guitar up hidden from sight. I would share my ideas about our project before the big surprise. If I waited long enough most of my peers would have made their way back inside.

We were going to build a solar system as detailed as possible with moving parts and lights for the stars and the moon. Sounds lame, right? Well, our project was going to be amazing. We had the choice: solar system or a model of an animal cell. Space was way more fun than cells, at least a little.

With my brains and Brittney's creativity, I knew we were going to make the best solar system ever. For the second time that day, I was so involved in my thoughts and plans for our project that I didn't hear Brittney behind me until she cleared her throat.

"Uh hum." I spun around to face her. As I did, I knocked all my research off the table, scattering it everywhere. Brittney set her tray down and dove to the ground with me snatching up the papers before the wind could blow them across the courtyard. Once more, I was mortified and hoped she didn't believe I was the world's biggest loser. Thankfully the folder covering the roses stayed in place.

As we finished picking up my notes, Brittney exclaimed, "Oh shoot, I forgot my sketches!"

"It's okay. We can use what I've got and look at yours tomorrow?" My hope was that we would spend more time talking about us, and less on the solar system. If she saved her materials for later, I could occupy her lunch time again the following day.

"No, really, I found some cool stuff you'll like. It'll take three minutes." Her fingers brushed my arm, my insides turned to jelly, and all I could do was smile. "Be back in a few," she said over her shoulder as she jogged back to the building.

Brittney had been gone for a minute, maybe two when I heard the thump of footsteps behind me. I was so engrossed in organizing my materials, I didn't realize the footsteps were way too loud to come from my dainty new friend.

"Hey, that was quick…" I started, but I was cut off by a voice that caused my blood to run cold.

"Hey, Jackson…what're you doing out here buddy? Why aren't you off by yourself watching the butterflies or weaving little crowns of grass?" I had been caught weaving flowers into crowns once and have regretted it ever since.

My body stiffened, but I didn't respond. If I pretended he wasn't there, maybe he would go, but my choice made the situation worse. Brett put his hand on my shoulder and squeezed tightly as he spun me around to face him.

"What? You think you've a shot with that pretty new girl? Not a chance." Brett's voice dripped with nastiness. For the life of me, I couldn't understand why people liked the guy so much. My guess was no one truly liked him; they feared him.

"Lo...look Brittney and I've got homework to do today so can you please leave me alone?" Being the kind, understanding guy he was, Brett pushed me hard in my chest forcing me to take a step backwards. My eyes frantically skimmed the schoolyard searching for help, but no adults were close by. I ran my hands through my hair, sucking back a cry of panic.

My distress intensified the joy Brett gained from causing me mental, physical, and emotional harm. The guy had problems. Later, I would find out how deep rooted his issues were; however, right then I didn't care.

"You think you can stop me?" he growled, stepping into my personal space. His voice grew lower, and his eyes zeroed in on me. He was dangerous.

"No Brett...all I want to do is sit, do my homework, and enjoy my lunch," I begged. At the mention of the word "lunch" Brett's eyes scanned my table and reached for the brown paper bag containing my food. Two seconds too late, I lunged for the bag, but Brett's hand wrapped around the brown paper parcel, and snatched it out of reach.

"What's this?" he asked dumping my lunch onto the grass. He ground my sandwich and chips under his foot, glaring at me the entire time, daring me to make a move. "Oops." He smiled. Behind me, I heard chuckling, and I realized a large group of our peers had formed a circle around us.

Great! Brittney would be back any second, and she would witness the whole stinking episode if I didn't stop the situation soon. As my mind wandered to where she was, I spotted her in the crowd. Her hands were clutched at her chest, the papers she had fetched crumpled in her fists. She looked from me to Brett, scared and confused.

Then, Brett noticed the roses which had become uncovered after he had snatched my lunch bag from the table. "Awe, look little Jackson has a girlfriend. Here doll," Brett said as he threw the roses at Brittney.

She took a few frightened steps back and didn't attempt to retrieve the sweet pink buds that landed at her feet. One of Brett's cronies found my guitar and strummed the strings back and forth with such violence I was afraid he would break them.

I. Saw. Red.

Humiliation filled my body at the thought of her witnessing this part of my life. Surely, she had heard rumors, but that was nothing compared to having a front row seat. If Brett continued the abuse, any chance I had with Brittney would be over.

She may not have known it, but it was written across her beautiful face. I had seen that look before. More than ever, I wanted to prove I wasn't the failure everyone thought I was, that Brittney was beginning to believe I was. Something inside me stirred.

"You know what? I changed my mind," I said between clenched teeth. Taking one large step towards him I leaned in. My face was inches from his, a tactic he had used against me many times.

In a matter of seconds, confusion, shock, and comprehension crossed his face; then, just as rapidly, those emotions were replaced with a look of glee—a look which reverberated fear throughout my body. Brett knew what I was going to do, and he was looking forward to it.

Wanting to make the first move, I swung my right fist with all my might, aiming for Brett's nose. There was so much force behind that swing, my lanky body spun clean around, then crumbled to the ground—right after my fist missed its mark. Brett had jumped back, a pretty basic move I hadn't accounted for. The crowd broke out in laughter. I scrambled to my feet knowing if I stayed down Brett would annihilate me. The only way to survive was to stay on my feet.

Enraged by the crowd's laughter, he grabbed me by the back of my head, and punched me straight on the nose. The pain was sharp, burning. I fell to my knees, my eyes watering so profusely I couldn't see. He pulled me back to my feet by the scruff of my neck. I stumbled around, blindly trying to grab anything sturdy to stabilize myself. Where were the cafeteria monitors? They had to see what was going on.

Dazed, I didn't consider defending myself any further. However, not taking any chances, Brett threw his fist into my stomach folding my body like an accordion. He then grabbed what was left of my lunch and rubbed it in my face. The chocolate cake Mom packed as a special treat was thrown with such force at the back of my head it stuck to my skull. The cake stayed there for several seconds before tumbling down my back, leaving a trail of thick fudgy icing along my spine. To shame me further, he took a can of soda, shook it up, and opened it in my face. The carbonated beverage burned my nose and eyes.

My spirit was broken, and all I could do was sit and wait out Brett's cruelty. I didn't attempt to stop him; I had given up. He won. There was no coming back from this.

Brett's assault lasted only a few more seconds before he decided to end his attack. It felt like hours. Each and every move he made lasted an eternity, etching itself into my mind. There would be no escaping the torment of that day.

Before he left, Brett bent down and whispered in my ear, "You may want to rethink coming back to school tomorrow…or ever. If you do, I may get a little more creative." As a final insult, he kicked dirt in my face as he walked away, his buddies laughing and pumping their fists in the air the entire time.

The degree of devastation was immeasurable. Sobs wracked my body as I cried uncontrollably. Tears streaming down my face, and saliva streaming from my mouth. Before the crowd broke up, many of them took pictures and video recordings of my meltdown. I drooped to my side, hugged my knees to my chest, and laid there for several minutes covered in soda, cake, dirt, and tears. I rocked from side to side crying so hard my throat burned, but my peers watched on.

Meanwhile, I could see the shoes of my classmates as they retreated, laughing and joking among one another as if they hadn't witnessed the abuse I suffered. Not one of them offered to help me, and I refused to get up until all were gone.

Don't get me wrong, there were some students who didn't laugh, who hung back wanting to help. After a moment's thought, they were too scared to go against Brett. Their fear caused them to leave me behind like a wounded dog.

I despised them, all of them, but what hurt the most was watching the tall brown boots I had admired that morning walk away. Away from me, and away from the carefully selected roses that still lay on the ground. Brittney walked away, moving quickly and with purpose—to get as far away from me as possible, her lunch tray still perched on the table untouched. Her callousness dried my tears and replaced them with a bitterness in my chest that spread throughout my body like wildfire.

Hatred entered my heart for the first time. I hoped it would stay there as a reminder to never care, to never trust again. At least then, I would never again feel the pain and hurt I now felt with the realization that I was a nothing, a no one. Strangely enough, all the torment I had gone through the last three years hadn't caused me the grief I felt right then.

Brittney's betrayal cast a shadow over my soul. I had expected it from Brett and the others, but not her—she was supposed to be different. Wasn't that cross around her neck a symbol of something good? Did it not indicate she was supposed to be better than those who stole my joy?

Once everyone had left, I stood up and brushed as much of the dirt and muck off as I could. Then I walked away, leaving my books, notes, even my beloved guitar sat on the ground, abandoned. Not caring what happened to any of it, I stumbled away like a zombie. A horror-stricken cafeteria aide rushed to my side.

"Oh no, what happened to you?" The poor woman's voice shook. She held her hand out to stop me, but I brushed past her.

"Wait, where are you going? We need to get you cleaned up and...and we need to tell someone..."

She called out for me to come back, but I ignored her and she didn't follow.

What the actual heck? Where was she when I was being brutalized? Maybe the school should hire more staff to monitor the place, I thought. Honestly, I didn't care. I didn't plan on returning, ever.

My anger carried me all the way home. I don't know how long it took to walk the few miles home, but it wasn't nearly long enough to suppress my rage. Fifty miles wouldn't have been long enough. Fortunately for me, no one was home when I got there. On Mondays, my mom volunteered at the hospital. She wasn't due home for several more hours, and Lilly was still at school. The last thing I wanted to do was explain to either one of them why I was covered in my lunch.

Careful not to make a mess of mom's floors, I went straight to the bathroom and ran water for a shower. While I waited for the water to heat, I looked at myself in the mirror. My eyes drooped into empty, dead pools of sorrow. The reflection staring back at me was a far cry from the confident boy who had been ready to take charge of his life earlier that morning.

It had taken years to figure out I was broken, but finally I knew. The fact no one wanted to befriend me was a big clue that I was seriously flawed. The one person who I had thought was a friend had been whisked away. I bowed my head and cried. I knew what I had to do.

Chapter Four

The person I saw staring back at me wasn't who I wanted to be.
Death shrouded my soul, how was I to know?
Oh, how was I to know that hate was ready to collect its toll

After my shower, I went back to the mirror and stared at my reflection. I stared so hard and for so long, I wasn't sure if the image reflecting back was even me. A stranger to myself. I began to question why I was alive.

Do I have a purpose on this planet? What would happen if I put an end to it all? My mind and the form staring back at me through the looking glass become detached from one another.

It was time, and there was much preparation to be done. I put on my nicest white button-up shirt, and a pair of navy slacks. It was my picture day outfit. I did, however, forgo the navy tie with tiny teal sail boats. I tousled my hair lightly with some of my mother's hair gel, and brushed my teeth, much like I had a few short hours before.

However, this time there was no excitement, no 'take my life back mentality' all of that was dead. My stomach let loose a large, gargling, grumble, filling the room. I was starving; after all, I had never gotten around to eating my lunch.

It couldn't hurt to eat last night's leftovers before…the end. The thought of mom's pot roast and mashed potatoes set my stomach off growling louder than before. My mouth was watering profusely by the time I pulled the food from the microwave. It seemed a strange thing to do, sit there eating leftovers, as if my world hadn't crashed down around me less than an hour ago.

The silence was deafening. Mechanically, I went to Mom's old record player and put on *Nearer my God to Thee*; the record was already on the player. The sweet melody of violins brought on the tears once again. Although a beautiful song, it always reminded me of loss. I let the tears flow as I chewed the delicious food my mother had prepared. I devoured the food before the song finished playing but didn't move until it was over.

Once finished, I removed the needle from the vinyl and stood in silence. I hoped that was how the end would be: silence. No more taunting or name calling. Just silence and peace for my mind and soul.

As a courtesy to my mother, I washed my dishes and put the leftover food away. At the thought of my mother, a pang of guilt jolted me back to myself, but it passed and I was once again lost, separated from reality. *It has to be done...I* briefly wondered if those were my own thoughts or if they stemmed from somewhere else, somewhere darker.

It would be hard for them, Mom and Lilly, but they would be better off without me. In my heart I knew that what I was about to do was wrong, but the real me was too far away. The hurting Jackson had taken the wheel and he was too powerful. The only thing he cared about was ending the pain.

Every few feet I stopped and studied the pictures Mom meticulously hung throughout the house. I studied each photograph, etching each memory into my mind. I wanted to take them with me wherever I ended up. Pictures of Lilly and myself hurt the most: at the circus, the park, and my favorite of us at the beach where she had buried me up to my neck with sand. If I was able to feel emotion in my afterlife, I would miss her like crazy. The thought of my sister was almost enough to change my mind, but the taunts and laughter of my peers replayed through my mind. *Brittney's retreating brown boots...*shame reared its mighty head and a wave of hatred washed over me.

I hoped Lilly and my mom wouldn't hurt for long. They were strong. Without a doubt, they could make it through anything. I was the weak one, just like my father, ready to flee my life instead of sticking it out. I despised my father for passing his weakness on to me. The mere thought of being anything like him confirmed what had to be done. My absence would save everyone so much heartache.

My father had left us a few years back for a new woman and her kids. Since then I'd been plagued with thoughts of being like him, a coward. *There is no doubt, I favor my father in looks and now apparently his personality as well.* He was a sorry excuse of a man, and that's what I believed I had become. *For years, I have been subject to my own weakness, but not today. Not ever again, my last act in this world will be to take complete control.* In that moment I perceived this as bravery.

In hindsight I wish there had been someone to talk to. I bet that person would've told me how stupid I was being. They would've told me I was an awesome person, that I deserved to live. They would've told me I was nothing like my selfish father. We would've shared our sorrows then talked about girls, watched scary movies, and ate junk food until we exploded. That would've changed everything. If I had had a friend…but there was no one, just Mom and Lilly.

Mom…she wouldn't understand. She loved me and would say anything to keep me with her. Mom is a special kind of person. Everyone loves her. She would never understand what it is like to be me. To be alone, hated, self-loathed. I don't want her to know what a loser I really am, especially after her disappointment in Dad. She would be devastated to know her son is the laughingstock of the school, that I am used as a punching bag by my classmates. It would be so embarrassing for her, for Lilly.

Lilly…Lilly is just too young. Talking to her about anything other than princesses and baby dolls is inconceivable. She still believes I am the coolest guy around. I hope she'll feel that way after I am gone. There will be a time when she will know her big brother was a colossal mess, but hopefully she can find it in her heart to love me still. I'd love to be the big brother she could look up to, but it isn't possible. I am nothing. These thoughts and others like it swam through my head until I realized time was of the essence.

It was growing late, and I had to get things in order if I was going to follow through with my plans. I didn't look at the clock to check the time; probably should've, but I wasn't thinking straight. My brain was filled with a thick fog; it controlled me and I wasn't even thinking for myself. My body was on autopilot, and I was going through the motions.

Robotically, I moved to the linen closet and grabbed a sheet—it belonged to an old set that was never used anymore. The sheet was covered in Teenage Mutant Ninja Turtles. I smiled sadly, wishing I could go back to the time when I was young enough for turtle sheets. Back when life was nothing more than an endless adventure filled with toys, imagination, and neighborhood friends.

I found Lilly's diary and pen and scribbled a note to my mother. It simply said: I can't anymore…I love you…I'm sorry. A lone tear ran down the tip of my nose and splashed onto the paper distorting my words, but it was legible. I left the note on the dining room table open where Mom would easily find it.

Sluggishly, I trudged up the stairs, my head hung so low my chin hit my chest. The chair I carried from the dining room was heavy. It belonged to an antique set once owned by my great grandmother. Wrestling it up the stairs took some doing, but I managed to maneuver it into my room. Once I had it in place in my closet doorway, I tied the sheet to a randomly placed ceiling hook in my closet. All of my life I had wondered why that hook was there. *Perhaps this is its true purpose.*

Tying the noose was tricky, my fingers were slick with sweat and shook violently. I wasn't sure if it were fear or fatigue from lugging the chair up a flight of stairs. Oddly, my body was reacting much differently than my mind. Finally, the noose was tied and loosely placed around my neck. I stood on the chair and leaned back ready to kick it away when a thought struck me. *What are people saying about today?* I removed the noose from my neck and hopped down from the chair.

My laptop was sitting on my desk. I flipped the lid and signed into MediaSpace, a media page that linked all of a person's social media to one site. Hungrily, I scrolled though post after post eager to see what people were saying about my altercation. My stomach flipped inside out; I almost lost my lunch. It was ugly.

At least twenty of my peers took it upon themselves to post pictures and videos of me during and after my fight with Brett. My fingers shook as I moved them over the finger pad of my laptop. It was sick, all those kids enjoying my pain. I hated them. If I didn't end my life soon, I would go insane. Dark thoughts spun through my mind, and if they didn't stop soon, I was afraid I would hurt someone besides myself.

One picture was taken after the cake had been thrown at the back of my head and was captioned, "Got Cake?" There were several comments that followed, making jokes. My classmates were real comedians.

Another photo caught me in an odd position of flailing about, right as Brett kicked dirt in my face. My mouth was wide open, and his foot wasn't visible (it had been cropped out) so it appeared as if I were shooting a cloud of dirt from my mouth. The photo was captioned, "Ladies and gentlemen, may I introduce to you, *The Rare Dirt Spewing Nerd of Melon Croft Middle.*"

There was even a photo of a chubby baby with cake all over his face next to a photo with me after Brett had thrown my cake at me titled "Who Wore it Better?"

People who never laid eyes on me were making fun of me. Adults were creating memes out of the worst moment of my life. It would get worse once the school day ended. I couldn't imagine what would happen once everyone got home and had full access to the internet. One guy hit the nail on the head when he said, 'If that were me, I'd rather die than to show my face again…what an embarrassment.'

I. Was. Done.

My vision blurred from tears welling in my eyes, but I refused to let them fall. I told myself my last moments on this earth wouldn't be spent crying over the cruelty of others. My last moments would be spent boldly looking death in the face. That was my irrational side talking. I now know there was nothing brave about what I did next.

Walking over to the window beside my bed, I tied the curtains back, and slid the glass open. I stuck my head out and felt a nice spring breeze blow by. It felt wonderful. I took a deep breath and closed my eyes for a moment, letting the sun warm my skin. Then I walked back to my closet and stood on the chair. I needed to make sure I could see our gardens from there. It was what I wanted to see as I left this world, one of the few things I found precious. I smiled: I could see it all, every flower, every plant in full bloom.

A voice in my head urged me to take the plunge before I lost my nerve.

I stuck my head through the brightly decorated ring, the turtles stuck in various ninja poses. It was awkward, twisting the sheet behind my head, but I got it. For a moment, I stood there looking at the room where I had spent most of my time, and said good-bye. A different voice, a very tiny voice, filled my mind telling me I didn't have to do this, that there was another way. I could live a good life. Surely life wouldn't always be this way.

I didn't want to hear that voice. I shut it down with one swift kick of my shoeless feet. The top-heavy chair fell over. My legs kicked and flailed. Immediately, my feet searched for a place to stand to relieve myself of the crushing pressure squeezing my throat. The floor was inches below; I couldn't reach.

It was only seconds of pain really, then the room began to dim. There was a ringing—I had thought it was in my mind, but then I heard Mom's voice. It was the answering machine she kept in her room. "Mrs. Liddle…I am sorry to inform you…an incident…we don't know where he went…"

Unable to breathe, I clawed at the sheet as it grew tighter around my neck. My throat gurgled and sputtered, fighting to pull fresh air into my lungs. Unsuccessfully, my fingers pried at the sheet, but I was powerless.

The feeling of regret was agonizing. Frantically, I grabbed for the chair, for anything to stabilize myself, desperately trying to stop what I had done. Unfortunately, I couldn't see the chair since I was unable to look around, and there was nothing close enough for me to grab.

My efforts were useless. The room grew darker, and I gave up the fight. It would only be a little longer. I let my arms hang listlessly at my side; they grew heavy as blood pooled in the tips of my fingers. I saw it—the light people talked about. Bright yellow like the sun—soft like baby's hair—

"Jackson, no, no, no, no." *Baby's hair…* my eyes popped open again. *Lilly!* My body began to spasm as I gave one last effort to free myself as my sister watched on. I twisted and swayed violently. Blood flooded to my head and a pressure like I had never felt pushed into my skull.

Lilly stood at my feet, holding a box of crayons, with a look of sheer terror on her face. An electric shock jolted my body. It was inconceivable. *Not Lilly! Lilly*…I cannot describe the sorrow—but in the blink of an eye it was over. Then it was lights out.

Chapter Five

The next few memories are scattered and broken. Hovering over the top of me were faces donned in surgical masks. "Jackson, Jackson, are you awake buddy? Hang on, okay," a voice said from above. I didn't recognize the voice, and I was a little confused about what he wanted me to hang on to. Stupidly, I grabbed at a ball of light hovering in front of my face. It was just out of reach.

"He's awake," a deep voice shouted across the room.

"Get him prepped. We're running out of time," was another man's terse reply.

For the life of me, I couldn't figure out where I was or why I was there. All I knew was I didn't have the ability to speak or move. All I could do was lay there and listen to frantic voices bounce from one side of the room to the other, like a fierce tennis match. A steady beeping kept rhythm overhead, but the noise didn't bother me, rather, it comforted me. I wanted to go back to sleep.

My mind shut down, then sprung back more aware of my surroundings. Above my head large screens monitored my heart rate and other vital signs. I wasn't sure what all the squiggly lines meant. Several clear plastic IV bags hung above my head. A few feet away a group of healthcare professionals huddled around a light box examining an x-ray.

My vision narrowed on them and everything around them disappeared. They were talking in hushed whispers and pointing to areas on the film. A brace had been wrapped around my neck prevented me from seeing exactly what they found so interesting. I wondered who the x-rays belonged to. The room dimmed again.

A sudden rush of movement woke me. It appeared the team had come up with a solution to their problem as their huddle broke apart and everyone scattered. One of the nurses slowly walked over to me and lowered a plastic mask to my face. It smelled funny, sweet and numbing. I couldn't hear the words she spoke, but I read her lips, 'count backwards from one hundred.'

I made it to ninety-eight before I was submerged into total darkness. When I awoke this time, however, I experienced a memory so vivid it has never dulled in my mind. I don't expect it ever will.

~*~

Darkness enveloped me like a cocoon. It didn't scare me necessarily, but I felt a distinct need to find light. My hunger for light was insatiable. I had to find it soon or surely I would shrivel up and die.

I felt…lost. The darkness bore down upon me; it pressed from all sides–black walls slowly closing in. Claustrophobia took control–my breathing became labored and a layer of sweat covered my brow. Mixed emotions were bottled inside of me ready to break loose. I screamed, but there was nothing–not even an echo. I was completely alone.

The only way to survive would be to break free from the blackness that had begun to snake itself through my entire being. I begged for help. From whom, I had no idea, but I hoped there was some force or god who would take mercy on me. My body crumpled to the inky blackened ground and I wept for help, to save me, or I most certainly would die. Someone must have been listening because my cries for help were finally answered. A tiny pinprick of light broke through the darkness giving me a sliver of hope.

I shot to my feet, wiped the tears from my face, and squinted, trying to determine if I was actually seeing what I thought I saw—or if the darkness had driven me insane. A miniscule speck of light in the far distance. After what must have been days of walking my legs weighed a hundred pounds each. I slid them one after the other towards that tiny beacon. My feet felt as if they were sludging through quick drying concrete. With each step, the speck of light grew just a fraction of a millimeter in diameter, but I continued on.

That growing glimmer of light filled my soul with hope; it was that hope that gave me the will to push on. Instantly, I was given a renewed sense of strength that allowed me to push on towards that breathtaking incandescence. As I continued to walk, the light grew brighter, gradually revealing a world around me. At some undetermined amount of time I was finally able to see the outline of trees and large rolling hills.

My eyes eagerly drank in all that the light offered me, and my body relaxed slightly. With a purpose I climbed the tallest hill I could find. The climb, although difficult, was well worth the effort. To be honest, there was nothing to do but walk until I was finally covered completely in breathtaking radiance. My initial reaction to the place, once I was able to see, must have been what Dorothy felt like when she discovered Oz.

Gratitude filled my heart as I stood there on top of the hill looking out around me, my eyes devouring the splendor of my surroundings. The hills were lush and the most beautiful shades of green. The trees were covered in leaves of every color imaginable, not just colors we are used to seeing on trees. I'm talking purples, reds, baby blues, and colors I am sure have never been seen on planet earth. This place was a dream.

As far as I could see there were gardens filled with vividly-colored flowers carved from precious stones. The sun glistened off the jewel-like petals, casting rainbows of color everywhere. That had to be my favorite part—seeing those colors cast all over the grounds, creating a lightshow across the land. The single most beautiful object I experienced was a cherry-tree with dainty petals that continuously rained from its branches to the emerald grass below.

The beauty didn't stop there. On the horizon, snowcapped mountains provided a breathtaking view. At the foot of the mountains, surrounded by ginormous palm trees, was a large body of crystal blue water, so clear I could see the outline of fishlike creatures swimming lazily through the refreshing waters. Closing my eyes, I imagined feeling the cool water flow over my skin.

The world was flawless, containing a perfect blend of everything nature had to offer. Its beauty was intense. There were no words to describe how wonderful it was. For me it was paradise. I had no idea how I got there, but I knew one thing—I never wanted to leave.

I lay my body down in the plush grass and soaked up the light which was offered by the sun. After spending so much time in the dark, I needed to take in the light. It warmed me, giving me a feeling of security. The warmth blanketed me and held me there in blissful, silent peace.

After having my fill of the precious, rich light, I decided to explore the land.

My mind wandered to what I should explore first. There were so many beautiful things to discover, and not one thing preventing me from doing so. I spent my first days exploring the land and becoming familiar with the place. High and low I searched for other forms of life, but mostly all I saw were brightly colored birds, although I did spot some female deer in a field once.

It was nice, being on my own. There was no one to talk to. For me that was fantastic—at first. In the beginning, there was no one I wanted to speak to. Besides, I really didn't remember much about my old life or about myself. I had no idea if there was anyone I wanted to talk to. It was perfect, or so I thought.

Don't get me wrong. Initially everything was flawless, until one afternoon I spotted a pillar of smoke rising in the distance. It was barely noticeable at first: just a tiny gray line of smoke, but over time the mass grew larger, darker, more ominous. It appeared the origin of the smoke was coming from the base of the snow-capped mountains. As much as I wanted to, I couldn't ignore the stack of smoke that behaved as a living being, breathing in the air around it. Believe me, I tried. Without a doubt, I knew I was going to have to hike over to the atrocity and see what was causing such unpleasantness in "my paradise."

The thought of confronting the problem introduced fear into my heart for the first time in my precious paradise. There was, however, a presence within me urging me on, reassuring me that I was protected, and all would be okay. Trusting that voice, I set out on my adventure.

My mind reeled over what I might find when I reached that lurid place. For some reason, I knew in my heart it had something to do with me. How I could have anything to do with that smoke, I didn't know. *Have I done something wrong?*

In all my exploring, I hadn't made it to the mountains yet. Uneasiness crept into my heart, my hands began to sweat, and my chest tightened. There was something terrible about that growing black pillar, something evil. Whatever it was struck fear in my heart. *How could my perfect place become infected?*

Anxiety hung around my neck like an anvil, just when I thought my body would snap in two from the sheer weight of it all, I heard a harp. Hearing anything other than the twitter of birds or the rustling of leaves in a cool breeze intrigued me. I didn't know how badly I had needed noise until it was there. The harps, although beautiful, didn't compare to the singing that soon followed. The words being sung were unintelligible, yet the sound tantalized the eardrum and soothed the soul.

My anxieties melted away, as my heart became overwhelmed with pure happiness due to the sweet melody of that heavenly tune. Slowly, as if in a trance, I followed the sounds until I came upon a small creek in the wooded area just off of my path. To my great surprise, there were people standing by the creek.

Actually, the only way to explain the beings is to say they were—like angels. The angels, clothed in long white robes trimmed in gold, shimmered when the sunlight broke through the trees. Their porcelain-like complexions were flawless, but it was hard to focus on what they looked like as their singing held me rapt. If they noticed my presence, it didn't disturb them as they sang. I found a patch of velvety moss to sit on, and leaned against a nearby tree, closing my eyes.

Slowly the music melted my anxieties away and penetrated my soul. I could've stayed there for an eternity, but eventually the music faded. When I opened my eyes, I was disappointed to see the angels had vanished. Initially, their rapid departure upset me, until I felt a power radiate from behind. I turned my head to see a Man watching me.

He looked different from the few pictures I'd been exposed to, but I knew Him. His eyes were kind, smiling, and an endless sea of gray. I was shocked to see Him standing before me. All I could do was stare back at Him dumbly for a long time, hundreds of thoughts flooding my mind. I tried to memorize his face, although most of it was hidden by a spectacular brown beard. The crinkles near his eyes were what I appreciated the most. They reminded me of laughter, and then I realized I missed that. When you live in a world by yourself there isn't much cause for a good laugh.

After I got over His sudden appearance, my first coherent thought was that I had gone mad. He chuckled, surprising me; I had never heard He had a sense of humor. If I had His job, I probably wouldn't have one. His chuckle also meant that He understood my thoughts. That scared me a little, as there was a lot of rubbish floating through my brain which I didn't want Him to see. But if the stories were true, He knew it all anyway. I cringed at the thought. It's one thing to know He knows and a complete other to *know He knows*. It's confusing I'll admit, but you'll understand one day.

Although He could read the darkness that plagued my heart, I was relieved to find He didn't hold it against me. Rather it seemed He expected to find me just as I was and loved me all the more for being me. It was strange meeting someone who knew every bit of bad that was in my heart and still wanted to be around me. Hopefully, my sinful nature wouldn't be a cause for me to leave this dear place.

"You fear; I see your darkness, but it's your light I desire. There is far more good inside of you, but you need my Father to show you the way."

He stood looking back at me with nothing but love shining in His eyes, maybe He would let me stay so I could find the way, the way to my goodness. He read my thoughts.

Shaking his head sadly, He spoke to me. "I know you would like to stay here forever, but you can't, my child," His eyes drooped with sadness. "Your time to live in paradise isn't yet here, and you may be surprised to know this isn't paradise." He gestured to the world around us.

"Where am I?" I asked.

"A safe place you created to protect yourself." He shared.

"Why would I…"

"All will be revealed to you in time," He answered.

"Okay," I said with a slight nod of my head. What else could I do? I mean this Man was—the boss.

"So, I'm not dead?" I asked. He shook his head. "But, I *am* here for a reason?" I questioned. He nodded his head prodding me to figure things out on my own. I wished I could remember—anything. "Does it have something to do with that black cloud of smoke?" I pointed towards the smokestack. I was shocked to see it had doubled in size and had the appearance of one of those five mile wide tornados that tear entire cities apart. Panic flooded my soul.

My eyes sought His to see if I was right. I knew He had the answers. His brow wrinkled for a second as He stared at the smoky area in the distance. Then He responded softly, "There are things that can ruin even the most beautifully tended garden. If we aren't careful, disease will come in and destroy all that is good."

He's talking about me…about my life. My life…

Then I doubled over as if all the air in my lungs had been sucker punched out of my body. I remembered. For the first time since I arrived in my 'perfect' place, I experienced the humiliation–pain–this place couldn't be paradise. In paradise I would never have to experience that kind of suffering.

A rush of emotions flooded my heart, ripping my soul to the point of physical pain. No wonder this world had been so appealing to me. No torture, no bullying, no people. I turned my eyes to the man who stood feet from me.

"Is this…what is this place?" I asked again. "And what does that cloud of smoke have to do with me?"

He looked over at the blackened area and nodded his head. "You can stop it, but you have to want to, and you will have to have unshakeable faith." He didn't provide the answer I was seeking but He provoked more questions.

Unshakeable faith…I don't know God or the Bible…stepping out on faith is going to be nearly impossible. A split second later I dropped my head into my hands burying my reddened face from view. *It is going to be hard, but I am going to have to control my thoughts.*

"Yes, child, you should control your mind, whether someone can hear your thoughts or not. This will make you strong in all things. A pure, strong mind will help you stop this monstrosity from destroying your heart."

I could only stare into His eyes briefly before I had to tear my gaze away. I wasn't worthy to look into His eyes. There was a power within Him I couldn't explain. An unbreakable love I wasn't ready to accept.

Confusion set in. "This is a place of rest for your mind, a place to escape your reality. It represents your soul. I need you to see there is much good and beauty here. Nourish your heart as you would this beautiful land, you will flourish. But I warn you, there are weeds that have already taken root."

He nodded to the black pillar of smoke. You will need to find a way to remove them before they spread and take over."

He spoke in riddles, I turned to ask Him what that meant, but He was gone. Yet, I felt His presence was near. I rose to my feet, suddenly aware of how rude I had been not to stand or bow at His feet or—something. *How is one supposed to act when they meet God or His Son...or are they the same?* It was confusing, I'd never been big into church, only attending the occasional Christmas service.

For the time being, I put those thoughts out of my mind as I formulated a plan on how best to make the journey to the smoky land. From what I observed over the last few days, there was a stone path which wound its way throughout the land. If I stayed along the path I was on, I would be able to pick fruit from the trees that lined the way. With the little stream running along the path as well, water would be no problem. The only thing concerning to me was a temperature change once I reached the snowcapped mountains. There wasn't much I could do about that except hope it was warmer at ground level.

Since I arrived, I had been clothed in plain beige robes no thicker than cheese cloth. The garments were like what the angels were wearing by the river, but mine weren't nearly as nice and they lacked the gold lining that sparkled in the sun.

Although His words scared me, they also encouraged me to press on with my quest. He assured me everything would be okay, hard but okay. Meeting my problems head-on seemed like a good way to start. I walked for a long time, my curiosity driving me further than I believed may be good for me. The sun and moon went through many cycles, yet I pushed on.

The cloud of smoke grew larger the closer I came. The behemoth made me feel smaller, more insignificant, with each step I took. Part of me wanted to run back to "my" part of the wonderland, back to the beauty and safety that I loved. Despite my fears, I had to stop that atrocity before it overtook the land or there would be nothing left to run to. For days, I continued on my journey feeling like I was Frodo Baggins in *The Lord of the Rings* with none of the excitement. My enemies, loneliness and doubt, bore down—suffocating me.

Tears filled my eyes when I reached the base of the mountain—patches of smoldering leaves and burnt flowers littered the ground. Where fruit laden trees once grew, blackened, twisted stumps remained. The ground was barren, charred. I could literally see the blackness spreading. Everything around me was lit with tiny flames slowly expanding outwards, consuming everything it touched.

If something wasn't done soon, the place I had come to love would be in complete ruin. Desperately, I searched for anything that could help me stop the ever-spreading devastation. There was no body of water close enough. My stream flowed into the sea a couple of miles back, and even if there had been water, I didn't have the means to carry any significant amount to put the flames out. The situation was hopeless. I didn't even know what the source of the fire was in order to determine how to extinguish it.

After much searching, I discovered a pool of what, at first glance, looked like water. After closer examination, I determined the body of fluid was less like water and more of a metallic black tar. The liquid sluggishly rose and pressed outward onto the land feeding the small fires. Not only did it feed the flames, but after closer inspection, it also played images across it's mystic-looking glass surface.

Peering into the substance I watched my life unfold as if watching a black and white movie. There were no happy memories being played.

The scenes that unfolded dropped me to my knees. Anger boiled inside of me and spewed out of my mouth in an angry rage befitting of the Hulk. It was me being beaten and humiliated by Brett. The cake, the words, the laughter…betrayal. Brittney...her boots…the roses. The hanging…Lilly.

The ebony fluid fed off of my sorrow and happily rose and spread, eating away at more of my precious land. The more distressed I became, the more gruesome the scenes developed. The pool of hate had to be created by the devil himself.

As my rage increased, more of the vile liquid spilled forward, spreading destruction. Screams of fury burst from my chest. I pounded the ground with my fists and tore tufts of charred ground. The liquid continued to rise at an alarming rate, and the small fires shot up into the air weaving black smoke into the smoky column, feeding its growth.

I yanked the hair on my head, turned my face to the sky, and cursed the Man who sent me to this place to relive all that pain again. That's when I was pushed back through the blackness into my real life where I awoke into my actual nightmare.

Chapter Six

It was then that I knew there was more to this world.
That there was something beyond what I'd ever known.
How was I to know?
How was I to know that you could save me from this world?

When my eyes opened again, I was in a hospital bed, scared and confused. My mind whirled, seeking answers, but for the life of me I couldn't figure what had happened. My mind had been erased of everything except for my dream.

I tried to push myself up, but I couldn't move. I called for help, but all that came from my mouth was distorted grunts. After a few frantic gurgling seconds I realized my arms and legs were tied down, and there was a tube down my throat.

Commence total freak out. My body jerked, hopped, and twisted on the mattress I was attached to. Although I couldn't see her at first, I heard my mother shouting frantically for help. Then I saw her pick up a white box about the size of a television remote and press a button.

"Please help! It's my son; he's having a seizure!"

"MMMMM," I tried to tell her I wasn't having a seizure—I didn't think I was anyway–however, all that came out was extraordinarily loud gagging. "HHHHHHHAAAGGGG!"

In seconds, a team of nurses ran in shouting over my body to one another, confusing me further. They ordered my mother out of the room—

she was too frantic, adding to the confusion. My heart beat like a jackhammer in my chest. If my adrenaline wasn't pumping I would've passed out.

"Hang on Jax," Mom cried out. "My son...my son," I heard her whimper as she was escorted from the room.

"Check his pupils! Rose, page Dr. Sanders we may have to...no wait...wait."

"Jackson?" A young nurse said peering down at me. I nodded my head, my chest rising rapidly up and down, up and down. My body was as tight as a guitar string. "Are you awake?" She shone a tiny light in my each of my eyes.

Another nod, my non-blinking eyes bulging out of their sockets. "He's awake and a little freaked out, guys. Jackson, you're okay...you're in the hospital. Nurse Rose is going to give you some medication to make you sleep."

"Guuurrllll," I tried to speak.

"No, just stay calm." She placed her hand on my chest. "You can't talk right now. Rose, go ahead." She tilted her head towards the I.V. pole near my head. An older woman walked up to my bedside and pulled a syringe out of her lab coat pocket.

"See, there you go," the older woman said. I shot her a menacing look before I felt my eyes roll in the back of my head.

Later, I learned episodes like that were repeated several times throughout the first part of my stay. Once my doctor felt confident I could breathe on my own, he had the tube removed from my throat. Losing the tube kept my freak outs to a minimum. There was comfort in being able to call out to my mother who stayed by my side to ease my mind. She rarely left me, just enough to care for Lilly.

"Mom, what happened?" I asked after waking from a drug induced stupor.

"Just rest, love," she said smoothing my ever-growing shaggy bangs from my forehead.

"Mom, please." I pleaded, jerking my head from her hands. I wasn't going to be put off any longer.

"Well...you attempted...you...hurt yourself," the words tumbled from her mouth like a nasty disease.

"Suicide?" I asked. *Why would I...*

"Apparently there was an incident at school with you and another boy," she answered through clenched teeth.

I shook my head trying to understand what or who would cause me to harm myself. I couldn't quite grasp it, the memory was just out of reach. My mind wouldn't allow me to touch it. Maybe it was for the best, after all something bad must have happened to cause me to take such drastic measures.

Mom and I had conversations like that off and on for days. The medication I was prescribed left me in a consistent state of drowsiness and forgetfulness. Over time, I discovered what happened the day I hung myself. Brett was the cause of my pain.

Mom skirted over some of the details, but what I pieced together was an ugly picture. Lilly had wandered into my room hunting for scissors to complete her homework when she spied me in the closet. She used the dining room chair to get to me, but she was too short so she climbed up the door frame with her feet and hands on each side of the doorway and cut me down.

She then ran downstairs to call 911, once done with them she went next door to let the neighbor, Mrs. Keller, know what had happened. Mrs. Keller tried reaching my mother, who was already en-route to the house because the school had tracked her down at the hospital. Mrs. Keller came to the house, loosened the noose, and started CPR while she waited on my mom and the ambulance.

By the time Mom had arrived, the house was filled with paramedics who had taken over Mrs. Keller's job of resuscitating me. They got a pulse back fairly quickly, but I was having a hard time breathing on my own. That's when they decided to intubate me, sticking a tube down my throat and attaching a bag they squeezed, forcing air into my lungs.

Once the paramedics had me strapped to a board, brace around my neck, and the tube down my throat, they loaded me into the ambulance. My sister had stayed behind with Mrs. Keller, and Mom climbed into the ambulance. I am sure she was totally freaking out.

What's truly amazing is my little sister had kept a calm head through the entire episode. If roles were reversed, I don't think I would've been as cool and collected as she was. If she hadn't acted so quickly, I would've surely died. At the time that's what I had wanted, but now I see what a travesty that would've been.

At the hospital, I was rushed to x-ray and had an MRI done, then the doctors made a game plan on how to proceed. Surgery was needed immediately, and at that point they didn't know if I'd survive.

I was rushed to the surgery wing where I was put under the knife for fifteen hours. Mom told me that was the worst time of her life. When I thought of what I had done to her, a tightness gripped my chest, even to this day. Hanging myself had a major impact on those around me, more so than I could've ever imagined.

My mother continued to explain that if Lilly hadn't found me, my air supply would've been cut off and eventually I would've died from lack of oxygen to my brain. There would've been no physical damage, I hadn't even broken my neck, but when my sister cut me down I was limp and fell at an angle, causing damage to my spine. I didn't blame her and never would. She was a seven-year-old kid trying to save her older brother. For the rest of my life, I would be grateful to her.

Initially, the surgeons had no idea how extensive my condition would be, only time would tell. The surgeons had repaired my vertebra with a steel rod and screws which they believed would heal well.

The real problem was the extensive damage done to the spinal cord from the fall. Doctors weren't optimistic about my recovery. The best course of action was to stabilize me and send me to the Manchester Spinal Institute which had more resources to handle my condition.

I ended up staying at the Institute for almost six months—the most difficult experience of my entire life. It was at the Institute where I had my freak-out episodes upon waking from my drug-induced coma.

"Mom," I asked sleepily.

"Hmmm," she replied.

"What's going to happen?" I asked, starting to nod off again.

"I don't know son, I don't know," was her answer.

Then I fell back to sleep. A lot of my days were like that, in the beginning. I would be awake long enough to get tidbits of information from my mother. Most of it she had to repeat because the drugs made me forget.

A lot of information was withheld from me those first few days in the hospital. About two days after I had been fully awake, I found out how much my life had truly changed. All day I complained to my mother how badly the restraints on my legs were bothering me. They felt like useless lumps of lead because the restraints had cut off blood flow to my feet. My mother never said much when I complained; she told me vaguely they would take care of it soon. In my naiveté, I thought my legs were still restrained even though the arm restraints had been removed when the throat tube was taken out.

The day I found out how extensive the damage was, I was in a pretty nasty mood. I caught the first nurse who walked into my room. She was older, short, and a little busty. She had taken care of me off and on since I had been there. I watched her pull tubes of medicine and syringes out of the pocket of her lab coat for a few minutes before I interrupted her.

"Excuse me, ma'am, but can you please take these restraints off of my ankles. They are way too tight and I can't feel my legs," I said gruffly.

The nurse—whose name tag said "Rose"—looked at me as if I had two heads. She opened her mouth to say something, then stopped, then opened her mouth again, but my mother stopped her.

"Ma'am, give me a moment to speak with my son please." The two women shared a knowing look. Then Rose nodded curtly and left the room, after making a production of picking up the syringes and putting them back in her pocket. I figured she would be back at some point, but I didn't really care. I was concerned with why my mother wanted to talk to me alone, and why she couldn't wait until the nurse was done doing what she had come to do.

"The medicine would've made you drowsy, and I want you to be fully awake right now," Mom said, reading my confusion.

Mom moved her chair closer to my bed and grabbed my hand. A wave of shock washed over my body as I observed the toll my situation had taken on her. Her eyes were cradled by deep black rings and she had lost weight on her already slender frame. Her normally well-groomed hair hung haphazardly around her head in clumps and tangles.

Guilt flooded my heart. My mother was a good woman; she didn't deserve this pain. The way her mouth quivered told me whatever it was which she was about to say was going to be bad.

"Jackson, what I have to tell you is going to be extremely hard to hear," she began in her teacher voice. Her lower jaw trembled, and tears coursed down her face. With her free hand she flicked the tears from her face. Her agony caused me pain. "When you…when you did what you did…"

Suicide, she couldn't say the word; I couldn't either. Mom paused for a second, trying to compose herself. My mother rarely cried, so when I saw tears trail down her face, terror bubbled from the depth of my stomach up to my chest. I said nothing as I waited patiently for my mother to tell me what she had to say.

She tried again. "When Lilly found you in your room, she…she cut you down." Mom let go of my hand, covering her mouth with her own, and sobbed.

"Mom, it's okay. Just breathe, and tell me…I need to know," I said. I grabbed Mom's hand again and gave it a reassuring squeeze. I needed to be brave for her, but I was failing miserably. She nodded her head, took a deep breath, and started again.

"It wasn't her fault you know just an—an accident." I nodded, encouraging her to continue. "When she cut you down, you fell at an odd angle and it caused damage to your spine. I don't understand all of it but…well… Jackson, you are paralyzed." And there it was.

I yanked the cover away from my legs and peered down at my feet. There were no restraints. The rubbery, flesh-covered extremities didn't look like my own. They just lay there worthlessly. I willed them to move with all the strength I could mentally muster, but nothing happened. I looked up at my mother. *Why wouldn't they move? No control…*

Her eyes bore into mine as she waited to see how I would absorb the news. I closed my eyes and laid my head back on my pillow. My ears rang, and my body felt light, as if I were floating.

A million questions flooded my mind, and I tried to get the answer to each of them from my mother. However, she didn't fully understand what was going to happen either. If I wanted definitive answers, I was going to have to wait for my doctor to come in and explain everything to me. Maybe it was for the best. I needed time to let the news sink in. But I knew one thing, I had made one horrific decision and it ruined my life indefinitely.

I didn't have much time to ponder my situation before the doctor came in to check on me. That very evening, as a matter of fact, I was introduced to him. "Knock, knock," he said as he entered my room. "Jackson Liddle?" He looked at my arm band to make sure I was who he thought I was.

Like I am going to get out of my bed and wander off. I nodded my head.

"It's good to see you awake finally. I'm Dr. Sanders, and I've been assigned to you until you're released from the hospital." Once again, I nodded looking down at my hands. His presence made everything real. I wanted to cry.

"I'm sure by now you've been told your diagnosis," he continued, looking at my chart and then intently at me. At that point I took a good look at him. He was a younger man, extremely tall, and beanpole skinny. But he had a kind smile that extended to his dark eyes. Wearing blue surgical scrubs and a white lab coat, he looked like a guy from one of the medical dramas my mom watched.

"Yeah," I said, my eyes tearing up. They were going to come no matter what I did. It seemed like I had been doing a lot of that lately, but I feared what Dr. Sanders had to tell me. He pulled a chair near my bed and leaned in close.

"Listen, kid, I know this is hard but I'll be here every step of the way. I have a plan set up for you and if you work hard you'll be fine. Life's going to be different, but you'll be fine. Got it?"

I studied him for several seconds, then I gave him the first real smile I had given anyone since entering the hospital. "I got it," I replied. Then I let out a barrage of questions which he was happy to answer.

In fact, he stayed with me for a good hour or more, explaining to me what happened to my body and what life would be like from that point on. I was fortunate that I could breathe on my own, as there are many people with spinal cord injuries who have to be on a ventilator—a machine that breathes for them—especially when they sleep. I had use of my body from the waist up and as long as I worked those muscles then I could do most activities I had done before, just with adjustments for my wheelchair.

My stomach twisted up thinking about what could've been: being stuck in a bed, not having use of my arms, not being able to cough without assistance. My life wasn't going to be the same, but it could've been much worse. I thought about what that meant for the greenhouse my mother and I had planned, but maybe we could figure something out.

The medical staff mentioned getting me an electric chair for later, but Mom and I decided a manual chair would be best to rebuild strength in my arms. Dr. Sanders also wanted me to start physical therapy to rebuild the strength I lost while lying in the bed at the hospital. It's amazing how quickly your muscles can break down if not used. It was going to take a while, but if I pushed myself, maybe life would be okay.

There were a multitude of daily activities I would have to relearn, but it sounded like my doctor had everything under control. He signed me up for a support group which I was less than thrilled about, but he felt it would help with depression and give me ideas on how to make my life easier—you know, tips and tricks from other chair-bound people. He also had a young woman named Dr. Todd who would come and talk to me. She would be my psychiatrist.

My doctor assigned a team of physical therapists to teach me how to care for myself. The simple tasks like bathing or reaching for something in a high cabinet would need to be relearned and would require special equipment when I returned home. Dr. Sanders urged me to give my all when it came to my plan of care, believing I could make as much of a recovery as possible for someone in my condition. At the time, I agreed to what he said, but I had no idea how difficult it was all going to be.

The very next day, in fact, I gave up halfway through my first physical therapy session. I had lost all motivation. My unhappiness continued throughout the day as I attempted to keep up with each nurse and therapist and whatever test or therapy they tried to perform. I was poked, prodded, scanned, stretched, and pulled like saltwater taffy.

And to top it off, I was expected to go to the support group Dr. Sanders roped me into. It was absurd to expect me to attend this group after the day I had, but I went. Against my better judgement, I went.

A nurse aid wheeled me down to the cafeteria which was mostly dark except for one corner that had a few overhead fluorescent lights slightly flickering. I felt like I was going to some highly secret society meeting no one knew about. I suppose that was a rather accurate description of the small group.

Everyone was already sitting in a circle, waiting on my arrival. The support group was small but diverse. In the group was a middle-aged black gentleman, a pretty girl around my age, a young guy—maybe in his late twenties, early thirties, and a girl around Lilly's age whose chair looked abnormally large for her tiny frame.

The older black gentleman wheeled over to me and placed his hand on my shoulder. "Jackson?" He asked. I nodded my head. "Nice to have you join us, son. I am Craig." His eyes were kind but below the surface was a deep…sadness, maybe. I figured it was because he was chair bound. I'm sure I had the same look in my own eyes.

"Thank you, my name is Jackson Liddle," I said, extending my hand.

"Pleasure to meet you," he flashed me a knowing smile.

"You too sir," I answered in my best attempt to be pleasant, which I might add was difficult to do considering the day I had just had.

What I really wanted to do was wheel myself back to my room and pass out cold in my bed. Unfortunately, I didn't have the strength to get back by myself. My night nurse had loaded me into my chair and brought me to the meeting. She wouldn't be back for an hour.

"Well, wheel yourself up to the circle and we'll get started. Everyone else is already here," Craig said.

I looked for the friendliest face in the circle, and wheeled myself next to the little girl. She looked up at me but said nothing. I gave her a reassuring smile, and she beamed back up at me with overly large toothy smile. The teen girl about my age looked angry and kept her arms crossed over her chest, staring straight ahead. Instantly, I thought of the young lady from *Great Expectations*, how haughty and proud she was. I also remember how enamored Pip was with her. Strangely, I understood his attraction.

She was beautiful, with long shiny auburn hair, perfect cheekbones, and a small heart shaped face. And then there was the younger guy who nodded at me and gave me a lopsided grin. I could tell by the mischievous smile he wore that he was a hoot.

"Well, let's get started. Jackson's new to the group so we're going to introduce ourselves, and if you feel like sharing your chair story you're free to do so. We need to make an effort to welcome Jackson into our group." Craig stared pointedly at the angry young girl. Her perfectly sculpted eyebrows shot halfway up her forehead before focusing her attention on the wall across the room once again.

Craig shook his head, and then continued, "I'll start, my name is Craig."

"C-dog," shouted the young guy with a chuckle. I stifled a laugh myself, it felt so normal being with other people who knew what I was going through.

Craig nodded, and then went on, "I've been in a chair for over ten years. When I was a young man, being a police officer was all I wanted to be." I studied his chair. It was well worn, with an iron-on police badge affixed to the back.

"For about twelve years, I worked the streets and loved it; that night was my last evening before I took an office job. I was getting older, slower, and I felt I would be of better use in other areas of the force." Craig stopped for a moment, his eyes staring off to some faraway place the rest of us couldn't see. We waited, the others in the group seeming to understand Craig's mental absence.

"Anyway," Craig came back to us with a slight shake of his head. "I was working the late shift, one of my co-workers called in sick. I was doing the normal rounds of the city and had to check some of the local shopping centers. When I got to the first strip mall, I noticed the back door to the sporting goods store was slightly open, so I crept up to the door and slid in. I didn't expect to see anything abnormal…maybe one of the employees forgot to lock the door—that kind of thing. It happens all the time. I didn't even call for backup."

The older man's eyes clouded with tears, but they never spilled over. "They were just kids, grabbing silly stuff—jerseys and shoes, they were probably going to sell them to make money to feed their families. We saw kids get busted all the time selling stolen goods to feed their younger siblings."

I almost missed the rest of his story as I pondered the life of the youth he described to me. "One of them snuck up behind me and pulled the trigger. I went down, accidentally firing my weapon, and shot one of them…he died instantly. The rest of the kids scattered. I realized right away I couldn't get up to chase them down. Something was wrong. The alarm wasn't set in the store, and I laid there for hours before help arrived—staring into the eyes of the young man I had killed."

Craig looked at me, there were no tears in his eyes, but the pain was evident. I must've looked horrified because he patted my shoulder and leaned over to ask if I was okay. I nodded my head.

"The kid missed my vital organs, but hit the spine right on, so here I am." Craig gestured to his chair, like he was the lady on Wheel of Fortune. I think he cut the rest of his story short to give others the chance to speak, or maybe it still hurt to talk about. Living through something like that would be devastating. It was strange though, it didn't seem like Craig was upset because he had gotten shot. I think he was more upset that he had killed someone.

For the next hour, I listened to everyone's "how I got my chair" story. It was sad, but I felt better knowing there were people who understood what I was going through.

Marv Georges was a pretty laid back fella. He had hurt himself while on his skateboard. At first glance he kind of looked like a young Brad Pitt, if Brad Pitt had long stringy hair and talked in a slow, lazy manner. Anyway, Marv was one of those people who didn't let his injury get the best of him. He was already doing tricks on his chair for public entertainment. I didn't know if I thought he was crazy or inspiring—maybe a little of both.

Val Henson told her story next. When I first saw her, I thought she was closer to Lilly's age but she was actually a few years older. Val, short for Valerie, was eleven but had a very tiny build. She had a bright toothy smile and her short black hair was cut in a neat bob. Val had been chair bound most of her life. She had had some kind of surgery as a kid and it didn't go well. That's all she shared so I don't know specifics. She was an upbeat and happy child. I liked her right away.

The exact opposite of Val was our little ray of sunshine (insert sarcasm here), Jessica Lowe, who took an instant disliking to me.

"I'm Jessica and I got ran over by a drunk driver, who happened to be my own dear dad," Jessica said simply, looking at me as if it were my fault. Believe me, if looks could kill I would be dead. At first I thought she was angry at the world, but really she despised me. This was easy to figure out when she turned to me and said, "You're an idiot!"

Dumbfounded, I continued to smile. *Is she speaking to me?* "The rest of us would do anything to have our legs back, yet you did this to yourself."

The smile plastered on my face slowly fell as comprehension dawned on me. She knew. I had no idea how she had found out, but she knew about what I'd done. The entire room sat in shocked silence, and then Craig, getting his wits about him, called the meeting to an end and quickly wheeled close to Jessica.

"Harsh, man," Marv said, looking over at Jessica with a pained look on his face, shaking his head in disappointment. Little Val took off, her little face fire red. She glared at Jessica on her way out.

Craig spoke in an urgent whisper to Jessica while she moved her hands wildly in the air. I didn't wait around to see what happened next; instead I wheeled myself to the hallway and found my nurse. Thank goodness, she was out there waiting on me. I would've died on the spot if I had to wait around with that lunatic on the loose.

Flaming mad, I swore I would never return to the group. Not only had that girl embarrassed me, she also made me realize my situation was the product of my own bad choices. And that wasn't something I was ready to accept.

~*~

For the rest of the week I pushed on but there was a part of me that couldn't put my all into what I was doing. My mind couldn't comprehend or focus on the commands, demands, and finally pleading of my therapy team to do what was expected of me.

Jessica's hate-filled words forced their way into my mind, repeating themselves over and over, floating through my head, invading my mind. Her words become a slow-moving poison, killing what little self-worth I had left. I unknowingly gave her control over me.

The group met weekly, but I decided I wasn't going back. I couldn't handle that spiteful girl. The fact that Jessica's words were true had a lot to do with that decision. I'd been stupid, and my diagnosis was preventable. By the end of the week, I couldn't decide if I was sorry for trying to kill myself or sorry I hadn't succeeded. In my mind, it was the world against Jackson.

My depression grew worse, and I was at my breaking point. The work was much harder than I had anticipated. The physical therapy alone wiped me out, not to mention my regular visits with my psychiatrist left me emotionally drained. It didn't take long for me to start running people out of my room, literally. Other than my mother, there were only two people I allowed to enter my room.

One of those people was Dr. Todd, my psychiatrist. I felt like she really "got" me, and she wouldn't put up with my shenanigans. And then there was Father Jim, the hospital priest. During his visits, I was able to forget about my useless extremities and the suffocating confinement of my room.

Originally, my doctor, a Christian man, had asked the hospital priest to visit me. He felt in addition to physical and emotional support, I needed spiritual healing as well. At first, I wasn't happy about that, mainly because I wasn't religious, but Father Jim was always fun to talk to. He didn't shove religion down my throat like I had expected a Priest to do. Most of the time, we just talked about music and gardening.

Father Jim was a kind, older gentleman—I would say he was in his late 60s, early 70s. However, it was hard to tell his age, because his face was rather youthful with few wrinkles. His head, covered with solid white hair, was the only thing that gave away his age.

It was Father Jim who convinced me to give the support group another chance.

"I don't care what anyone says, I refuse to go near that evil creature again," I said, pouting like a three-year-old.

"Try to see where she's coming from. She's upset about her own situation and wants someone to blame. Of course, she can blame her father, but he's locked behind bars for a long time. Her anger prevents her from visiting him, so she finds others to throw her frustrations at," Father Jim said.

"Do you know her?" I asked, rolling my eyes.

"I do, and believe it or not, she's a great girl, she's just hurting," Father Jim said. "There are things about her you may not understand, but you two have a lot in common." I scoffed at his words. "No, it's true," he insisted. "However, I would suggest keeping a distance until she has a chance to adjust to you. She knows what you did, but she doesn't know why."

"It doesn't give her the right—" I started.

Father Jim cut me off. "Of course not, but all she sees is a boy who had everything going for him and he ended it with one selfish—"

This time I cut Father Jim off. "But that's not true," I cried. If I had the ability I would've probably thrown myself to the floor and kicked my feet about.

"Yes, but she doesn't know that, Jackson. From the outside, your situation seems strange. Be patient with Jessica. I imagine you two can learn a lot from each other," he said.

I nodded my head, agreeing to give it a try. "How did she know, though?" I asked.

"I don't know; maybe she knows people at your school…" Father Jim shook his head.

"Hmm, maybe," I said, puckering my mouth.

Suddenly, I wanted to know more about Jessica, if only to see what she and I may have had in common and how she found out about my–accident. I decided to talk with Dr. Todd and see if she had any insight.

Sometimes I gave Dr. Todd a hard time, but she never gave up. However, no matter how hard she was trying I wouldn't talk about the day I had hung myself. But she pressed on. She did get me to open up about the events leading up to that day, but the day itself remained locked inside me.

Actually, to be fair, most days Dr. Todd didn't even ask about the bullying, but dug deeper into my past. She talked to me about how my father had left for another family, and how I felt lost without him. Honestly, there were aspects of my life that upset me which I never really thought about anymore, but they were still there. We also talked about Mom and Lilly a lot, and how I had let them down. Dr. Todd really helped me work through the hardest time of my life.

So, the next time Dr. Todd and I met we did talk about Jessica. I hoped she would have some special words of wisdom to win Jessica over, so I could be a part of the support group without once again becoming the victim of bullying. However, Dr. Todd pretty much said the same thing as Father Jim did: be patient and stay out of her way.

That's what I decided to do. I was determined to keep my distance the next time I saw Jessica, and then, over time, I would try to befriend her. However, this proved to be difficult because the very next time I attended a meeting, Jessica went at me again.

"You don't belong here," she said furiously as she wheeled her chair right up to me. The anger shining in her eyes was disturbing.

"Why not?" I asked heatedly. *Why am I always the one she targets?* This girl hated me from the beginning, and she didn't know a thing about me. I wondered if I had a sign hanging on my back saying, "Treat me horribly. I just love it!" *Will I ever escape this kind of treatment?*

"The rest of us are here because we had no choice, but you? You chose to be this way," she spat. Her words cut me to the core, but I couldn't help but envision how beautiful she might have been if she let her anger go.

"What do you know about it?" I asked, my voice starting to shake. I was doing all I could not to cry. I hated confrontation.

"I know you did this to yourself. What? Did the world get too hard for you? Mommy and daddy tell you "no" and you wanted to pay them back? Guess what? It's about to get much worse and the only person you have to blame is yourself." She was right, but I wasn't in a place to admit it.

"No wonder your dad ran you over," my words rumbled from my chest. "Too bad he didn't do us all a favor and finish the job."

I instantly wished I hadn't said the words but it was too late. She was so quick I didn't even see it coming. THWACK, right across my face with her hand. She then turned her chair around and wheeled off to Craig. I went the other way towards the elevators to see if my nurse had left yet. She had, so, completely worn out, I wheeled myself back to my room. I had gone through enough without having to deal with that lunatic.

As I was leaving, I heard Craig call for me, but I didn't turn around, I had no desire to listen to what he had to say. I was so mad that if I went back, I knew I would say terrible things and I didn't want to do that to anyone else. I just knew that beautiful demon was going to be a cause of great misery for me.

Part of my assumption was correct. I was miserable most of the time, but it wasn't all because of Jessica—although I threw blame her way as often as possible. However, I did have some pretty good times. As a matter of fact, my most treasured times in the hospital revolved around Father Jim.

The highlight of my day was seeing Father Jim walk into my room. The first time we had met, I remember thinking there was something special about him. He stood in the doorway of my room, his bright blue eyes sparkling with kindness and laughter. He seemed like he really loved life, making him the exact opposite of me.

Father Jim was one of those people you instantly became drawn to. He quickly turned into the father figure I desperately needed in my life. I wished my own father had been like him. Over time, I came to love him like family and he felt the same way about me.

The best way to explain it was that Father Jim brought the good out in me. He made me want to be good. However, when he wasn't around for a few days I acted terribly, and when Father Jim found out how badly I had acted, he wasn't happy. Honestly, it had been an accident he had found out I was acting up in the first place.

"Get out now," I screamed, as I banged my lunch tray against my bedside table slinging green beans all over my freshly made bed. My nurse had been trying to get me ready for physical therapy and I didn't want any part of it.

"Listen, kid, you have to—" my nurse started.

"No, you listen, lady. I don't have to do crap. You touch me one more time and I'll sue you so quick," I snarled, pushing my bedside table so hard everything on it toppled to the ground.

"You know what, *little boy*," the nurse snarled, putting emphasis on the little boy part. "Just sit here in your green bean mess then. If you decide to act your age, *then* we can talk. You know how to press the nurse button when you're ready," she shot her words over her shoulder as she walked out the door in a huff. Angrily, I picked up the soggy vegetables and threw them at the wall.

Father Jim happened to overhear this little tirade, and decided to stick his head in. I could tell he was unhappy with me by his over-exaggerated frown and wrinkled up forehead. "Jackson, I'm disappointed in what I just heard," he said. His normally bright eyes had lost their sheen.

"Sorry," I said trying to look pitiful. "I'm having a bad day."

"Don't be sorry to me, but your nurse could use an apology. I can understand bad days, but that's no reason to treat someone in that manner," Father Jim said sternly.

"You're right, I'll try to be better. I promise," I said. At the time, I really meant it, but the key word was, *try*.

Nonetheless, I tried to do what was expected of me. At least for a few days, or maybe it was a day and a half— come to think of it, it could've just been six hours. I mean, it was a start, right?

Never in my wildest dreams would I have thought therapy would be so difficult, but let me assure you, it was challenging. Learning to get things which were out of reach was a huge pain, I wanted to stand up so badly. A few times, I tried and ended up flat on my face. Having no control over my legs was foreign and frustrating.

If you want to have some idea of what I went through, just sit where you are and focus your mind on making your nails grow. Or you can try to make your hair stand on end. Then, keep trying, day in and day out. Seriously, that's what it feels like for me when I am trying to make my paralyzed limbs move. No. Control.

Getting myself in and out of my chair or in and out of my bed drove me crazy and took forever. I had to use my upper body strength to slide along a board from one place to another. Since I had been dormant for so long, my muscles were weak, and I had a hard time building them back up. It was exhausting. Of course, if I am being honest with myself, had I not been a complete brat, it all would've gone much smoother. It would have still been difficult, but much, much smoother.

Every single day I fought a battle mentally and emotionally which sometimes left me wishing I had died in my closet. In the beginning, I stayed angry a lot, but Father Jim helped immensely. That period of my life was like a roller coaster. One moment I loved life and felt positive; the next I was in a rage, causing everyone grief.

Many days, I blamed God for what happened to me—that is, when I actually acknowledged His existence. Once, and only once, I made the mistake of blaming God in front of Father Jim upon which he scolded me for fifteen minutes on my attitude, saying I was blessed to even be alive, blah, blah, blah. When he wasn't looking, I would roll my eyes, but I humored the old man.

I was convinced there was no way God existed. Yet, I frequently thought of the garden dream from when I was in my medically induced coma. I couldn't get the man from the garden out of my head, the one whom I knew to be God's Son. There wasn't a day that went by where I didn't get flashes of the garden. But that was only a dream; I told myself there was no way it was real.

Chapter Seven

Denial stole your love from me; I allowed it to fester.
If only I had let it set me free.
How was I to know?
How was I to know You could set me free?

My life was a vicious cycle of emotions, therapy, and self-reflection. After several weeks of being stuck in the hospital I felt trapped and alone. None of my classmates ever came to see me—not that I had expected anyone to. I was sure someone from my support group would've visited, but they were probably afraid of how Jessica would react.

Actually, since the day had I snapped at her, she hadn't even tried to talk to me. For the most part, she acted as if I didn't exist. That was fine by me. I didn't need people like her in my life, but I did wish there was someone my age to talk to. Then Brittney came back into my life.

I was completely distraught when I saw her face peer around the door frame. For several seconds, I didn't know what to say. Anger filled my heart, but the emotion that took the driver seat to anger was sheer embarrassment.

Embarrassed, that I lay before her in a hospital bed, broken and vulnerable. However, the worst emotion I felt when Brittney strolled into my room that day was shame. Isn't it funny, she abandoned me, yet I was the one who felt ashamed? Ashamed I gave those kids the power to upset me so much I attempted suicide, ashamed I trusted this girl so completely with my heart.

"Hey," Brittney said softly, taking a few steps into my room. The tiny space became much smaller. It was hard to breathe, as if her very presence sucked all the air out of the room. She looked down at her feet. I didn't know if she had a hard time looking at me because I looked so terrible, or because she felt bad for leaving me like she had.

Since I'd been in the hospital, I had lost some serious weight from the meds I was on because they suppressed my appetite. Not to mention, I didn't even try to make myself look attractive. My hair was stood on end, and I hadn't been at all concerned about hygiene that day.

"Hey," I said back, equally self-conscious. "Why are you here?" I was in no mood to beat around the bush.

"I wanted to see you," she said, barely above a whisper, still not meeting my eyes. That was fine by me. I was afraid of what my heart might do if I looked into hers.

"Any particular reason why you waited five months to come for a 'visit'?" I used my fingers to make the smarty pants quotation marks.

"I had to see you!" she almost yelled, pounding her fist on the nightstand by my bed. Her outburst made me jump—well, the top half of my body jumped; the lower half kept me grounded. She'd been so soft spoken up until that point; I wasn't expecting so much emotion to come from her.

Brittney's reaction must have taken her by surprise as well, because her cheeks turned a brilliant shade of red and she mumbled what I assumed was an apology.

"For?" I asked as if I was talking to a slow person. I was being cruel, but I didn't care. I needed to hear her say it.

"I wanted to say… I am so sorry for…not being there for you. I got scared and I…" Her mouth moved, but no sound came out. It was evident she hadn't thought about what she was going to say before she saw me.

"Embarrassed, maybe?" I finished for her. She started to shake her head no, but stopped and nodded her head in agreement. *Well at least she is honest…I guess?*

"Don't worry about it, I mean who needs friends?" I said. "Most of my life I've been friendless. I'm used to it!"

"We all need someone," she said. "You have to know people at school are talking about how sorry they are they hurt you all this time." She looked right at me and said softly, "I'm sorry I hurt you." The look in her eyes crushed my heart. I wanted to throw her out of my room, and I wanted to grab her and hold her close. I was so mixed up when it came to this girl.

Instead of doing either of those things, I said coolly, "No really, it's okay. It's not like you and I were real friends anyway. We were forced to work together. I bet neither one of us would've even looked the other's way if we hadn't had the misfortune to be science partners."

She stood like a deer caught in headlights; she had no idea what to say. She played with the cross necklace around her neck. Seeing the symbol made me angry. People like her made me sick, wearing a cross around her neck as if she lived the lifestyle of one who wished to be good. Yet she was the same as everyone else who had hurt me.

"Can you leave?" I finally shot at her, my patience wearing thin.

Brittney's face crinkled in the worst cry face possible, and she sobbed so loudly I grew embarrassed. Had she not been so loud, I would've felt slightly bad for her. Unfortunately for her, I was in a particular nasty mood and felt nothing.

"Can I visit again sometime? Maybe when you have time to…to forgive me?" she asked.

The girl was desperate. I stared straight ahead, shook my head, and pointed to the door.

Brittney attempted, unsuccessfully, to stifle a sob as she ran out of the room.

A twinge of guilt crept into my psyche but it faded.

As soon as she was gone, I looked into the hallway and spotted Jessica sitting in her chair. She stared at me as a pensive look fell over her face. Without her normal scowl, she looked as pretty as I had thought she might. The moment she realized my eyes were on her, she wheeled away down the hall. I started to shout how rude it was to eavesdrop on someone, but just then another visitor popped into my room.

The first time Father Jim caught me being mean, he was a bit understanding, but this time was different. It was the first time I ever observed true frustration from him, his face slowly reddening. "Friend of yours?" he asked.

I gave him a good ol' shoulder shrug. He had caught me being a super-sized jerk, and I wasn't happy about it. So, to save face, I told myself I didn't have to justify my actions to him, he wasn't my real father.

I didn't have the time or the desire to be scolded by Father Jim. There were bigger things on my mind, like figuring out why Jessica was stalking my room. She was no longer a patient at the hospital so she had no reason to be there, especially on my floor outside of my room.

"Your mom's a gardener, right?" Father Jim interrupted my thoughts, switching gears. I nodded my head in response. "You enjoy working in the garden, correct?" Father Jim asked. Another slight nod, but I still refused to look at him.

"Well then, I'll tell you this in a way that may make sense to you. Hatred grows like a weed in the middle of a beautiful garden. If the weed isn't removed quickly, it will spread and ruin all it touches."

It was his tone, more than his words that caused my head to snap in his direction. For a moment, I expected to see the Man from my dreams standing in the room with us. But we were alone. Father Jim didn't seem to notice my strange behavior, as he kept right on with his little speech, pacing the floor with his hands clenched behind his back.

"If you don't remove the weed, it will spread, killing everything beautiful and good in the garden." Goose bumps ran up my arms; I saw the garden of my dreams so vividly.

"Jackson, do you believe in God?" This was the first time Father Jim had come right out and asked me. I had expected him to ask eventually, but it caught me off guard that day. Father Jim received another shrug of my shoulders. I was instantly on the defense, with my arms crossed over my body. But, inwardly, I despised the nasty smirk on my face. I knew I was acting like a toddler, and that I would regret it, yet I couldn't seem to stop myself.

"I don't need you here, you know. I did just fine before I met you." The lie filled the room. We both knew I did not do well before he came into my life, but he was kind enough not to say it out loud.

"I see," he said with a slight nod of his head, his face drooping into an uncharacteristic frown. And that was it. He stayed with me for only a few more minutes before he excused himself. I was mortified by my behavior, but not enough to counteract my teenage pride.

My behavior that day cost me a major setback. Before then, there was talk about me going home. I had been progressing quite nicely at learning the basics on how to care for myself, but I ruined it by going into full jerk mode for like the fiftieth time, and refusing to do what I was supposed to. It was self-sabotage at its best.

In the span of one day, in a moment of stubborn weakness, I had completely reverted back to how I had been acting: running staff out of my room and not doing the work required of me. Most days I sat in my bed and did absolutely nothing. No matter what anyone said or did, all I would do was stare out the window for hours, watch TV, or sleep. Once, after I missed a few support group meetings, Craig came snooping around to see how I was doing. It must have been the cop in him wanting to investigate the case of the *Missing Wheelchair-Bound Teen*. While he was there I pretended to be asleep. He waited for over an hour before he left.

Seriously, I was in total creep mode. However, my behavior didn't last long. This time, someone squealed. A nurse talked to my mom and told her about my shenanigans. Actually, I was surprised they allowed my behavior to go on for so long.

When my mother found out, she stomped into my room and shut the door. Her eyes narrowed on me. Instantly my palms started to sweat and my heart pounded. I had no idea why I was so scared; it must have been the flames shooting from her eyes and smoke billowing from her ears.

"Hey mom–" I started but she cut me off.

"How dare you!" Her voice thundered through the room. I'm pretty sure the windows vibrated just decibels from shattering into a million pieces.

"Wha…" but then I got it.

She knew. If my mother had ever displayed that kind of rage before, I had never seen it, but I caught it that day. She put me in my place using what she likes to call 'tough love' but what I call 'fear for my life'. She must have stopped by the nurses' station where they gave her a report on how I'd been behaving.

"How selfish are you really, Jackson?" My mother's chest heaved in and out as she stood by my bed towering over me. I was scared to death. The Incredible Hulk himself would be less scary than my mother.

"I—" but she cut me off again. This wasn't going to end well for me.

"Not only do you put me through the single worst experience of my life, but you deliberately cause a huge stink in this hospital. All because you don't want to do what needs to be done for your health." She emphasized each you and your with a quick jab into my upper chest with her razor sharp index finger. I was one poke away from impalement.

She took a short pause to breathe and then went right back at me. "I mean, really, do you think these people are here because of their poor decisions? No, they are here to help you with yours." She pointed her finger right between my eyes. If she were to poke my skull just then, I knew her finger would go straight to my brain.

My mother's round face surpassed violent red and headed straight to eggplant purple. "Right now, we should be packing you up and taking you home." At this she turned and started to pace the floor.

"Every single day Lilly cries for you! She misses you being home, but what do you do?"

This was a rhetorical question so I didn't say a word. She was far from done tearing into me. "You sit up here like you're king of the world, and everyone should tiptoe around you, to make your life easier while you make everyone else's harder." Her eyes scanned the room. For a moment, I was scared she was looking for something to throw at me.

"How could you? Really, how could you act like those bullies you so despise?" she asked, as she plopped down in the chair across the room from me. She must have felt we should have a little distance between us. I agreed.

At this point, she stopped and laid her head into her trembling hands. Her words brought me back to reality. The fact that I had been acting like my aggressors never crossed my mind. I wondered at how I could change so rapidly. Then I thought once again of my garden dream. How quickly I had let hatred and anger into my heart, and how rapidly I had let it ruin my life.

The shame that had been plaguing me became all-consuming. I hung my head and cried. Tears streamed down my face as remorse for my behavior flooded through me; not only was I a victim to bullies, but I was a victim of my own terrible actions.

I got so lost in my world of self-pity that I didn't hear Mom stand up and walk over to me. She wrapped her arms around my shoulders and we sat that way for a long time, our sobs ricocheting off the hospital room walls.

Chapter Eight

After Mom left that night, I lay awake in my bed thinking about my actions. I questioned myself and everything I had done. *Is this the person I want to be? Who do I even want to be?* The person I had become wasn't who I wanted to be. I didn't want to become like Brett, or the many other people who tormented me, but I couldn't go back to who I was either. I mean, really, if I had been happy with the guy I was before, I wouldn't have tried to kill him. The realization that life is messy had hit me hard, and I needed to clean mine up.

With as much determination as I could muster, I decided I was going to be the kind of guy who worked hard, didn't run away from problems, and wasn't a bully. For the next week, I did everything the doctors and nurses said. Every person who came into my room was pleasantly surprised with my change of attitude. Some of the staff thought my abrupt change in behavior was a cruel joke, that at any moment I was going to snap back into crazy Jackson mode.

For the first time ever, I pushed myself to the limit, which was much farther than I ever believed possible. Without a doubt, I was getting better and each day my strength improved. My change in behavior encouraged the staff to work with me more, and they pushed me to work harder. Most days they didn't have to bribe me with candy to get up and do my work. Even Dr. Todd was pleasantly surprised with my improvement when I rolled into her office for a visit.

"Hello, Jackson, how are you?" She asked, smiling at me.

"Hey," I said happily, eating a candy bar the nurse brought for me as a gift for good behavior. "I'm good."

"Well, that's wonderful. You certainly look better than when I saw you last week." She eyed me carefully, probably making sure I wasn't up to something.

"Last week, we talked about you opening up and talking about the day you hung yourself. Have you thought more about that?" she asked.

"Well…yes," I said, licking chocolate off of my fingers. "But, I still don't feel like talking about it."

"Oh, I see…" Dr. Todd said, the light in her eyes going out. I could tell she was disappointed.

"But I did write it all down for you," I said slyly.

That got her attention. Her head shot up, and she looked hopeful. "Really?" she asked. I nodded and pulled the letter out of the notebook which I had stuffed under my leg.

"Here," I said, handing her my story. "Just read it later when we're not together," I asked.

"Sure, no problem," she said, carefully filing my papers into her toffee-colored briefcase.

"Oh, and check it out," I wheeled back to the door and lifted the heavy black case that held my beloved guitar.

Dr. Todd clapped her hands excitedly, her eyes lighting up. "Oh, you got it! Will you play for me?"

"Um, sure," I looked away embarrassed. "But just a little, I'm rusty and haven't had a chance to practice yet.

"Okay." She sat back in her chair.

I strummed the strings a few times making sure it was tuned, and then quickly found my groove. My fingers floated across the strings in a light melody which I had been working on before I went into the hospital. I didn't have words to the song yet, but they had been forming in my mind slowly since I'd been in the hospital. I played for a few minutes, then set my guitar down in the unused chair next to me.

"That was amazing, Jackson. I had no idea you were so talented."

"Oh, um, thanks. It's just something I mess around with. Nothing major." I shrugged.

"Well, I for one think you should keep at it. You have amazing potential there."

"Thanks." I blushed, and Dr. Todd moved on.

"So do you want to tell me why you're being so cooperative all of a sudden?"

There was my Dr. Todd. She didn't beat around the bush at all. For the next hour, I told her about my near death experience with my mother, the run-in with Brittney, my poor behavior with Father Jim, my mixed feelings about Jessica, and how the support group had been going.

That was the first time Dr. Todd had heard about Brittney, and she had a lot of ideas about what may have happened to cause Brittney to act the way she had. But I wasn't ready to cut Brittney any slack, so I blocked out most of her advice on my lady problems.

Then Dr. Todd took the opportunity to segue into my falling out with Father Jim. "We all make mistakes, but the key to growth is owning up to them when we make them."

I was slightly surprised she knew about what had happened before I had told her, but then again, Father Jim knew everyone in the hospital so it made sense that they would have talked.

"You know, Jackson, Father Jim really does care for you," Dr. Todd said.

"How do you know?" I asked.

"Well, he told me," she said simply.

"What else did he say about me?" I was eager to know if Father Jim was angry with me.

"How about you ask him yourself. He would love to see you," Dr. Todd answered gently.

"Yeah, maybe," I said, suddenly finding the cuticle of my nails extremely interesting. I felt conflicted; part of me wanted to see Father Jim, even if it meant I had to apologize, but the other part wanted to simply let things go and hope the problem would go away on its own. I never like admitting it when I am wrong.

"What should I do about Jessica?" I asked.

"As to that, Jackson, I have no good advice," Dr. Todd replied. "Maybe you and Jessica will never get along, or maybe ten years from now I will be attending your wedding," she kidded. Dr. Todd was a downright riot some days.

"Yeah, fat chance of that happening, the girl is a complete loon." I smiled at Dr. Todd. The mere thought of me and Jessica being anything other than mortal enemies was pretty funny.

"Well…you never know, but seriously, Jackson, it sounds like Jessica has been through a pretty rough time. I seem to know someone else who gives other people a hard time when he gets upset about his condition," she added cleverly. She was so slick, I didn't even realize she was talking about me until after she had left. Chuckling to myself, I concluded that a higher power had to be involved when they assigned Dr. Todd to my case.

Dr. Todd helped me see my behavior was no different than anyone else I encountered. I myself had been a bully like Brett, a quitter like my father, and a selfish brat like Jessica. I even gave up on those I cared about, just like Brittney. As I sat and mulled that over in my mind, I began to understand what Father Jim had told me about forgiveness and about realizing we all have faults.

Chapter Nine

I worked hard for another week and on Friday, Dr. Sanders finally signed my release to go home. He came in to talk with me about what to expect when I went home.

"I'm really proud of you, Jackson, for stepping up and working so hard to get well," he said.

"Thank you," I answered cautiously. I knew there was a lecture coming.

"When you get home, things are going to be tough for a bit. You won't have staff to wait on you hand and foot. Now, I've already talked to your mother, and she knows she needs to show some tough love to keep you on track," he said sternly.

"What...what do you mean?" I asked.

"I mean, your mom isn't your nurse or your maid, so don't treat her that way. And you can't be freaking out on your family like you did to my staff." I squirmed uncomfortably in my bed.

"Ah, you thought I didn't know, huh?" Dr. Sanders asked.

"Well, I was hoping you didn't," I said honestly. He laughed good-naturedly.

"I know everything that goes on in my part of the hospital, but my staff is used to that kind of behavior. Everyone in your position goes through a bad spell as they try to adjust to a new life. The tricky part is not reverting back to that place," Dr. Sanders said. "You're a strong kid. Don't let your situation destroy you, okay?" He patted my arm with his hand.

"I won't...I promise," I said. His words of concern made me feel a little nervous. Deep down, I was scared of going back to that dark place, of being that terrible person I'd been a few weeks prior.

Dr. Sanders must have picked up on my apprehension, because he tried to ease my worries. "Your mom has been working with home health to get all the equipment you'll need at home. You have nothing to worry about."

Unfortunately, this only worried me more. Not only was I afraid that my mother's beautiful home would be tainted by all the equipment scattered around, but I was also concerned about how expensive it would be to remodel the house to accommodate me. I was upset at the idea of mom having a hard time paying for it all, but she refused to talk to me about money issues, so all I could do was hope things went smoothly.

My big return home was scheduled for the following Monday. My mother used that time to prepare our home for my arrival. The doctors wanted to do some last-minute tests and checkups before I was discharged, giving her time to work everything out.

My doctor also wanted the physical therapy team to go over some vital information with me on how to care for myself at home. I was eager to leave, but I understood a few more days could help me better cope with what I would face. I was really going to miss the Institute. The staff here had become like family to me, even if I had behaved like a little devil most of my stay.

To my surprise Father Jim came for a Saturday visit which made me extremely happy. He hadn't been to see me for over two weeks, since the day I had treated him and Brittney so poorly. Those two weeks were torture for me. I had been worried my attitude had negatively affected our relationship indefinitely. I have a feeling Dr. Todd may have had something to do with Father Jim's visit, but she'd never admit it.

Father Jim walked into my room, his normal cheery self, and we had a really nice time. It wasn't until the end of our visit when he even mentioned my behavior.

"Jackson, I know you are going through a hard time, but I really want to talk to you about how you let your situation affect you," he began. "The reason I visited you so frequently is because I care a great deal about you. Also, I know you're hurting and I know without a doubt you need God."

My mouth dropped open in protest, but he held his hand up to silence me. "I know you're confused and conflicted and you've gone through a terrible ordeal. However, the things you've gone through aren't of God. Believe me, I know where you're coming from. I've been in a dark place myself."

"Really?" I was skeptical. I couldn't imagine Father Jim experiencing even a small fraction of what I had.

"Oh yes, very much so. There are circumstances in my life that will trouble me until I die," Father Jim said. His eyes glazed over briefly as he thought about his past. "Believe it or not, I haven't always been a man of God. But even if I had always had a relationship with Him, I would have still gone through trials. Being a Christian doesn't magically make our life in this world easy, but it does ensure that after our time on Earth is over, we'll have a glorious time in Heaven for eternity." He looked as if he really believed what he was saying.

I couldn't help thinking the poor guy was looking forward to something that would never happen, with a God who wasn't real.

"How can you be sure? How can you believe in something you can't see, touch, or feel?" I asked. It might sound like I was being condescending, but I wasn't. I really wanted to know how Father Jim could believe in a God that allowed so much chaos in a world He had created.

"Well, because I can see Him and feel Him, and although I can't touch Him, He has touched me...here." He put his wrinkled hand over his heart.

At this point, I know I was giving him the "man, you're crazy in the head" look. He chuckled at my puzzlement but continued to explain.

"You see, I can see Christ through His loyal followers, and I feel Him when the Holy Spirit fills me with His love. He touches my heart with His mercy and the miracles He performs every single day."

I was still confused about how Father Jim had so much trust in a God he couldn't see, but I knew he meant well by telling me what he believed.

However, I had to be honest with him at this point. "Father Jim, what do you want from me? I can't feed into this—religious...stuff."

I was trying to be understanding, but really, I was tired of feeling like I was wrong for not believing the same as him. After all I'd been through, I didn't think I could ever give my trust to a God who would allow such bad things to happen.

"Jackson, all I want is for you to give me a chance to share Christ's love with you. He can bring you peace." Father Jim looked me directly in the eyes, and what he said next really caught my attention. "Before I go too far with you on this, I want you to do something for me."

He reached into the inside pocket of his blazer and pulled out an envelope. "All I want you to do is read this letter. That's it." His demeanor was serious, and I knew whatever was in the letter was important to him.

"Now I know you're going home and you'll be busy adjusting, so all I ask is you read this when you have time. When you're ready, give me a call. I'll come for a visit and we can talk."

My love for Father Jim pushed me to give him a chance. Reluctantly, I grabbed the letter from his outstretched hand. Besides, I was a bit eager to do anything I could to close the rift I had caused in our relationship.

We spent several more minutes catching up before Father Jim excused himself. "Well, I best be off, Jackson. Take care and if you need someone to talk to, give me a call and I'll be there in a flash." He lightly patted my hand with his.

"Okay, Father Jim," I said. "Thanks," I added as an afterthought. We gave each other a final wave good-bye and just as he was about to walk out the door, I cried out for him. Quickly, he stepped back into my room.

"I'm...sorry...I was terrible. I had no reason to take my anger out on you." My cheeks grew hot and tears stung my eyes.

Father Jim walked over to me, gave me a hug, and then he said the words I needed to hear. "It's okay, son. I forgive you. I forgive and love you no matter what."

My garbled sobs were muffled as I gave in to his embrace. I held on to him, afraid to let go in case he never came back, like my real father. We sat that way until I broke away and gave him a shy smile. Suddenly, I felt vulnerable. Father Jim hung back for a few more minutes making sure I was okay before he left.

Carefully, I set his letter on my bedside table, too tired to read it. It had been an emotional day and I was completely wiped out. As usual, sleep was hard to come by as the army of nurses, doctors, and therapists paraded in and out of my room to give me last minute advice.

It was nice to have guests—even if they were paid staff—but I really needed time alone. I tossed and turned all night, thinking about God, my attitude, and what Father Jim had said. Even when I did manage to dose off, somehow my garden dream got all mixed in with everything else, giving me a fitful sleep.

Despite the rough night, Sunday morning came quicker than anticipated. I was glad it was Sunday. The hospital was a little quieter than during the week. I normally didn't see my physical therapists or Dr. Todd on Sundays. However, Dr. Todd stopped by to have a small chat and see if I was prepared to go home.

"Good news Jackson, we have it all worked out for me to see you weekly. The first session, I'll come to your home and just assess how you're doing. From then on out you'll see me in my satellite office closer to your home."

That was good news to me. Ever since we found out I was going home, my mother had to fight with the insurance company on everything that was needed for my care. It was frustrating, watching the stress stack against her.

Dr. Todd didn't stay long. As she was leaving, Dr. Sanders dropped in to see if I had any last-minute questions. "Is there anything you need or anything we can do to make your transition easier?"

"No, I think I'm good," I said.

"Well, we're going to run a few more tests to make sure everything is a go for Monday, but as far as I can see, you'll be getting an eviction notice from me ASAP."

"You know part of me hates to go," I said with a laugh. "Had you told me a few months back I would say those words, I would have said you're crazy."

"I know what you mean. Oh by the way, Craig is having a special meeting tonight, and I really think you should attend."

Shaking my head, I said, "I really don't want to…"

"It would be good for you. Do it as a favor to me?" Dr. Sanders raised his eyebrows in question.

I started to resist, but I gave in. I could suffer through one more run-in with Jessica if I had to. "Alright, I'll go."

"Good. Well Jackson, I probably won't see you until your two-week follow-up, but I'll come by before you leave. If you need anything…don't hesitate to reach out."

"I'll let the nurses know," I smiled at him. Every time he stopped in, he always made sure I knew he was there for me if I needed him.

"You got it. See you in a few weeks!" He said.

"See ya then," I said back.

"Don't forget the support group meeting tonight," he called over his shoulder.

"I won't," I called after him, amused that he once again talked me into another dreaded meeting where I had to share the same air as Jessica, the spawn of Satan.

~*~

When I arrived at the meeting, I was surprised to see no one was there. There was a long table laden with piles of finger foods and a gigantic cake in the middle. Slowly, I wheeled up to the table. Written on the cake were the words "Good Luck Jackson, We'll Miss You," written across it. I was touched, but wondered where everyone was. Then from behind me, I heard Marv and Val arguing playfully about who should get the first piece of cake.

"No way, kid. I'm older. I should get the first piece," Marv said.

"Have you ever heard of ladies first, Marv?" Val retorted, giggling her tiny head off.

"Nope…Hey, Jackson, uhhh surprise, I guess," Marv said, the same mischievous grin he wore about ninety percent of the time sprawled across his face.

"Hey, guys…is this for me?" I asked, stunned.

"Yeah, Craig wanted to do something for you since he knows you won't be able to make the trip up here each week," Marv replied with a smile.

"Wow, that's really nice. Where's Craig?" I asked.

"He, uh, went to call Jessica," Marv said, avoiding my eyes.

"Oh, she probably doesn't want to be here, huh?" I asked.

"Well, it's different with Jess, ya know, man," Marv said trying to be a peacemaker.

"Yeah, she's a spoiled rotten brat," Val said. I agreed with her but didn't voice my opinion.

For a few moments, we all sat there awkwardly in silence, until Craig wheeled in. "Hey Jackson, how are you, my brother?" he asked, wheeling close enough to give me a quick handshake and a pat on the shoulder.

"I'm good. Just excited to be going home, ya know," I said.

"I do know. All of us here know all too well the excitement that comes with getting out of the hospital," he said kindly. My small group of friends nodded their heads in agreement. I smiled, hoping one day I could mean as much to others as they meant to me.

"I am going to miss you all," I said. Then I thought of Jessica, the girl who would forever hate me. "Most of you anyways."

Craig caught what I meant. "Don't be too hard on the girl, Jackson. She only knows pieces of your story, and it confuses her." I knew he was trying to be fair to Jessica, but I felt like he was scolding me too.

"You know you're right," I said as something dawned on me.

"What's that?" Craig asked, a confused smile creeping up his face.

"I've never told you guys my 'chair story'," I said.

"You don't have to, Jackson," Craig said gently.

"No, it's time. I need to tell someone…you guys will get it…I think," so for the next hour I told my story as we all munched on chips and finger sandwiches. Craig, Val, and Marv were good listeners, and I started to feel like maybe it wasn't so bad to be a part of a group of people who understood what I was going through.

When I was done telling my story, Val came to me and put her hand on mine. "Jackson, you'll never have to worry about being alone again. You have us, always." Her touch and kind words meant a lot to me, and I realized she was right. I'd met so many supportive people who had become permanent fixtures in my life.

Craig, Val, Marv, and I all hung out just talking and laughing for a long time that night. It was great. I had finally found…friends.

We all shared stories about ourselves, and I wished I'd opened up to them earlier. Maybe I could talk my mom into bringing me back for meetings from time to time.

As our group broke up for the night, I looked over near the elevators and saw the back end of a wheelchair round the corner away from us. I only caught a flash, but I thought I recognized the familiar shiny locks of a pretty brunette before she was gone.

Quickly, I wheeled myself into the hallway to see if I could catch her, but no luck. I shook my head and wheeled myself to the elevator. Women—they were another mystery of the world I didn't even want to try and understand.

~*~

Since I'd had so many visitors over the weekend, I hadn't thought much about what life would be like away from the hospital. Once back in my room, I became a bundle of nerves, scared of what my life would be like without all of my hospital helpers. Until that night, I didn't realize how dependent I'd become on the staff. I knew Home Health would be coming by to help out, but I already knew it wasn't going to be the same as what I had in the hospital.

Not seeing my mother much over the weekend caused some uneasiness as well, but I knew she was busy getting the house ready. I hoped she didn't have to change it too much to accommodate me. As eager as I was to get home, I wanted time to slow down just a little so I could ready myself for the changes that were to come.

It seemed I had just blinked and the weekend was over. My mother had arrived to pick me up. I was already sitting nervously in my chair, dressed in khakis, a button-up shirt, and my hair slicked tightly to my scalp. I felt like a dweeb, but I was too wound up to care. My stomach was in knots, bile bubbled in my belly. I was trying to be brave and make the best of the day.

Mom's face lit with excitement as she entered my room. I never realized how deep her love for me was. It's funny how little you appreciate someone else's love for you, but when disaster strikes, you see what was right in front of you the whole time. I mean, I say I love a lot of things, pizza…candy… but the love my mother has shown me through all of my troubles—well, there are no words to describe it. The only thing I wished was I'd never put my mother in a position to have to show me her love like that. I should've just known, and it should've been enough to prevent me from harming myself.

My selfishness put a strain on my mother in many ways, physically and financially for sure. This was made evident when she wheeled me downstairs to a brand spanking new white van she had bought to accommodate my chair. Mom explained that when I was ready, it had the capability to allow me to drive with the use of hand controls. That was exciting, knowing that soon I would be able to drive, and my condition wouldn't prevent me from that. It was the first thing I found I could do like a normal teenager. My feelings were bittersweet though as I knew a van like that cost a lot, and we didn't have extra money lying around.

"Jackson, I know what you're thinking and it'll be okay," mom said.

"But this had to cost a lot mom." Sadly, I looked at just another example of how badly I'd messed up.

"It did cost a lot, and unfortunately I had to use our greenhouse funds for it. But we'll start over on our savings, and one day we will have our greenhouse."

My heart sank. We both wanted that greenhouse. She worked so hard to save for that. I started to hate myself all over again.

"Don't be hard on yourself, Jackson. We would've needed a new car soon anyway. The Toyota has seen better days. Besides, I saw plans for a greenhouse that was much more cost effective with more space. In no time we'll be spending our days growing fruits, vegetables, and plants that no one has ever seen before."

I smiled, picturing myself in the greenhouse working hard, maybe using it as a safe place to sing some new songs. Then I thought about the garden from my dream. I wondered if I could cultivate plants like I'd seen there. That would be amazing. Trees that rained pastel colored jewel leaves. Where would I even start?

"Yeah, that would be cool," I said, still feeling bad about the money.

Mom was a retired school teacher. Over the years she saved and invested well, giving her the ability to retire at an early age to be home with me and Lilly. Then, life had changed when our father left.

After he abandoned us to make a new family with someone else, he paid the bare minimum in child support and that was all my mother had to go on. Yet, here I was, being lifted into a brand spanking new van she had to pay for because I made a huge horrible mistake.

I also realized how taxing it was for her to help me into the vehicle and put my chair up. That was something I was going to ask my physical therapist to help me work on ASAP. I really didn't want my mother to have to suffer because of my mistakes. My anxiety grew as I realized we hadn't even pulled out of the hospital parking lot and I had already discovered something else I needed to work on.

Once we were finally loaded in the van and on our way home, my stress diminished a little—although I felt strange being away from the hospital. It was as if the hospital was my safe zone. I assumed that was normal considering I had been there for almost six months. It was spring when I went in; now it was mid-October and the trees were full of beautiful, colorful leaves. Of course the beauty I was looking at now couldn't compare to what I had experienced in my dream, but it was still nice to see the outside world again.

The day was so inviting, I rolled down the window and hung my head out. It felt good to have the wind blow through my hair, my cheeks jiggling like jello. I closed my eyes, pretending I was flying.

"Jackson, get your head back in the car right now! I'm just getting you out of the hospital, I don't want to take you back because you went and got your head severed five miles down the road," Mom said sternly, but with a smile.

"Mom, it's fine! Geez, I haven't been out of the hospital for months. I want some fresh air," I complained.

"Yeah, well you can get plenty of air without hanging your head out the window. What if a big semi comes along and rips your head clean off?"

"How's that even possible? You're driving in the slow lane!" Unless someone passed in the emergency lane, my head was going to stay safely attached to my neck. "Seriously, the worst thing that could happen is a bug flying down my throat."

Mom laughed louder than anticipated for my weak attempt at a joke, but I figured she was anxious to get me home. After that, she calmed down, but I had a feeling she would be smothery for a while. I couldn't blame her. She loved Lilly and me. I'm sure she wanted to keep us around as long as possible.

"Okay, okay…it just feels so nice," I said. Mom nodded her head as she watched the road. Really, it was a beautiful day.

The sun shone in through my window and warmed my skin. I felt alive and wanted to get out of the van and run up and down the street—until I realized I'd never be able to walk, run, or jump again, which pretty well bummed me out. That was normal for me nowadays; I would start to feel almost normal, then a harsh reminder of my limitations would rain down upon me.

Depression could really kill a good mood. I guess that makes sense. Dr. Todd would tell me to find the positive in my situation, but right now I wanted to be all gloom and doom. Part of that was my condition and part of it was being a teenager.

The drive from the hospital to our house was a long one, and it took around an hour and a half to get home. I had a long time to think about how miserable I was. I was also reminded how often Mom had to make the trip back and forth to take care of me and to be with Lilly. Mentally, I was on a roller coaster, my moods up and down, backwards, forwards, and sideways. One minute I was up, the next I was feeling bad for something I had put my loved ones through. It didn't help that Mom was talking a mile a minute when all I wanted was quiet time to think things through.

We were almost home, when Mom finally let out why she was so excited. If I hadn't been so hung up on myself, I would've noticed she was talking more than usual which indicated she was hiding something. "Jackson…" she started.

"Hmmmm?" I was half listening.

"When we get home I have a few surprises for you." I turned to look at her and she was about to explode. My mother was horrible at keeping secrets.

"I'm listening." I perked up…What? We all like surprises.

"Well, I am not going to spoil them all, but I want to warn you we'll have a guest or two at the house to visit. The only reason I am telling you is

I know you've been moody lately, and no matter how you feel when we get home, I want you to be kind to everyone." She was still smiling, but there was an edge to her smile that said, 'You mess this up and you will wish you hadn't, buddy'. I had no intentions of messing up the surprise. The anticipation of who may be in wait for me actually lifted my spirits.

Mom was so excited I was really going to try to not disappoint her. Not to mention, I was truly excited to see who was at my house waiting for me. That was the million-dollar question. I had no friends, and we had virtually no family in the immediate area. Considering the fact my dad couldn't be bothered to come to the hospital not even once in the six months I was there, I didn't anticipate him being on the guest list. Mom wouldn't have been so chipper if Dad was going to be around. I had no idea who would even want to see me. It was a good thing Mom hadn't told me an hour and a half ago or I would've died of curiosity.

We finally pulled into the driveway of our house. Seeing my home never felt so good. My eyes drank in the place where I spent most of my life. I loved our house. We lived in a nice gated community in a stone, two-story home with a lot of character. Everyone who visited always commented on it, saying it looked like a cottage out of a fairy tale. The stony paths, tiny koi fish pond, and brilliantly flourishing gardens that filled most of the yard had a lot to do with its charm.

Mom pushed me to the house. Normally, I would've fought her off to do it myself, but the drive had taken a lot out of me. Also, I was excited to see my visitors so I wanted to get inside as quickly as possible. Before we got to the door, I noticed someone had built a ramp leading to the front door for my chair to go up.

Whoever built it did a great job. The ramp looked like a cobble stone bridge that ran over top of the newly expanded koi fish pond. They even lined it with more flowers and bushes to keep it from being so noticeable. It was beautiful, but it made me feel another pang of guilt because I knew work like that cost money.

My guilt was quickly replaced by excitement as Mom unlocked the door and wheeled me over the threshold. The house was dark at first but once we were all the way inside, someone flipped on the lights. Several shouts of "surprise" greeted me.

Although I knew there would be a few people there, I was stunned nonetheless seeing all the bodies that filled our home. My eyes scanned the room to get a good look at who was there, but I was instantly pounced on and almost suffocated by a small blond-headed being.

"Jackson! I missed you!" Lilly squeezed the air out of me. Folding her in my arms, I sat there and held her.

Mom didn't want to let Lilly visit much at the hospital, because it caused her to have bad dreams. Not seeing Lilly hurt us both. I missed her something fierce and obviously she missed me too. For a long time, I held her, attempting to hold back the sobs (unsuccessfully I might add). I wished I could've held off until our guests went home.

But my sister had saved my life and ensured I got a second chance. I owed a lot to my little sister, and I hoped one day I could repay her for what she'd done for me. As I held her, I realized how much I had messed up that day. There's nothing I regretted more than the decision I had made to end it all. As I held my sister close I knew there was so very much I had to live for.

The room went silent as my guests watched my homecoming. Lilly and I broke apart and I looked up. There wasn't a dry eye in the place. Mom held her hand over her heart, tears gleaming in her eyes as well.

Looking at the people in the small crowd, I spotted many of my "friends" from the hospital. There was my physical therapist—Josh, a young guy fresh out of college, and Dr. Todd. She looked very pretty in jeans and a tee shirt, a nice change from her crisp business suits. Father Jim was there, his eyes shining with love. There was Nurse Rose and a few other people from the hospital whose names I couldn't remember, including a handful of nurse's assistants. Even Craig made an appearance. Several of my guests rushed me at the same time to congratulate me on my hard work in the hospital and to welcome me home.

It was a nice little party. My mom ran around playing hostess, serving trays of sandwiches and desserts. As I was settling in talking to my guests, I noticed my mom disappeared for a few minutes to answer the doorbell.

I couldn't even fathom who else would come to visit because everyone I knew was already in the room with me. However, I was wrong. I did know the person who walked into the room. The fact that she had the nerve to come to my welcome home party gave me the biggest surprise of all that day—a much-unwelcomed surprise.

Chapter Ten

There were days when I didn't understand why you tested me.
How could I fight; the pain wounded me like a dull knife.
Weren't you sent to protect my life?
How was I to know?
How was I to know you had a plan?

The person who followed my mother into the room looked almost as uncomfortable to be there as I was uncomfortable to see her. Brittney slinked in looking, well…beautiful as always, but I could tell she wasn't happy about being there. Father Jim caught my eye from across the room and I could tell he was concerned, but he watched from afar as Mom ushered Brittney right up to me.

"Jackson, here's your friend, Brittney. Aren't you happy to see her?" Mom was so eager to believe I actually had a friend. I had never shared with her how Brittney had broken my heart. "I ran into Brittney and her mother at the store last night, so I invited her over," Mom gushed. She was so excited to make my homecoming a special event I didn't have the heart to ruin the moment.

"Yes, Brittney, how are you?" I plastered a fake smile on my face while my mom stood gawking at us. My blood began to boil. How could she show up here and ruin my homecoming?

The moment my mother walked away to tend to our other guests I dropped the nice boy act. "Why are you here?" I asked through clenched teeth.

"I wanted to see if you still felt the same way you did in the hospital? I want you to know how sorry I am." The tears that built up in her eyes made me angry. I could handle the water works from my mom but not from Brittney. I mean, was this girl for real? I was about to tell Brittney exactly how I felt, when Father Jim strolled up to me and interrupted us.

"Excuse me, I hate to interrupt, but Jackson—I was wondering if you could show me your mother's rose garden. I heard she has the prettiest garden around this area. In fact, it's quite famous in the gardening world." He gave Brittney an apologetic smile.

"Yes, Father Jim, I don't mind at all. As a matter of fact I could use some fresh air. Brittney, if you will excuse me," I added coolly. She said nothing, but slowly backed away. She must have left shortly after, because I didn't see her again that evening.

"Thanks, Father Jim. I'm afraid some wounds still need time to heal," I said, maybe a smidge ashamed of my behavior. Father Jim pushed me out the back door so we could admire Mom's roses.

"Yes, I could see that, Jackson. All I want to say is… try to find a way to deal with your anger. You know there's a way…"

Great, now he was going to start the God stuff again. But he didn't. Instead, he patted my shoulder and walked off to join the other guests. I stayed outside to think.

A short while later Mom found me still on the back porch staring at the roses. "Jackson, are you okay?" she asked, her face furrowed in concern. I knew she was afraid something bad would happen now that we were away from the hospital. I wasn't the only one dependent on the hospital staff.

"Yeah," I smiled at her. "I'm just… getting sleepy. I haven't had this much activity in a long time. It's nice to see the fall roses," I said with a reassuring smile. "I missed this…" I nodded my head towards the gardens even though there weren't nearly as many live plants as there were before I went into the hospital.

"I know, from now on we'll make time for you to get outside more. There is a carpenter coming next week to build a ramp back here so you can work in the garden when you feel like it." Mom said as she smoothed my hair down on one side.

More money, my face fell in disappointment. Mom picked up on it quickly. "No, listen; I got a great deal. The man who is going to build it is doing me a huge favor in exchange for landscaping his new home. It is a great trade for me."

"Well…yeah I guess," I said, slightly relieved.

"Alright, we have one more surprise for you and then you can rest. You think you can handle that?" mom asked.

Her worry was covered by that sneaky smile of hers. This surprise must be really good, because she looked as if she couldn't contain herself much longer. Normally, my mother was the world's worst at keeping secrets. Every Christmas she ended up giving Lilly and me half of our presents early because she couldn't wait until Christmas Day to give us gifts. In her defense, she's a pretty good gift giver.

"Okay, everyone." Mom clapped her hands, as we re-entered the room. "Jackson's starting to get a little wore down, and I think it is time for him to go *lay down*." She emphasized the "lay down" part quite loudly.

She seemed way too happy to send me to bed. "Jackson, I've something to show you, but I want you to know everyone here had a hand in this."

I looked at my mother quizzically. I couldn't fathom what she could be talking about. Mom was behind me at this point and pushing me down the hall, bypassing the stairs that would normally have taken me to my bedroom. She kept on going until we stopped at the spare room/office. She opened the door and as she wheeled me in, my jaw dropped.

For years the room was a huge mess, a "catch all' for our family's odds and ends, stuff we rarely used. My skateboard, our skis, sleds, things we used infrequently had been stacked up in two of the four corners for as long as I could remember. Mom furnished the room with a spare bed and an old computer perched on a rickety computer desk for any guests that came for a visit.

However, the room I was led into looked nothing like the space I remembered. It had been completely remodeled for me. There were no words to describe how I felt when I saw all the hard work that had been done. I was literally blown away.

A state-of-the-art type of air mattress that prevented bed sores with a remote-controlled base that would raise the head and feet of the bed up and down was in the far corner. The mattress itself was fitted with brand new bedding in shades of gray and yellow.

In the opposite corner was a new computer for me to catch up with my school work. The walls were painted a medium gray color and old school records hung in a diamond pattern on one wall. On the opposite wall someone had stenciled a guitar in bright yellow. The artwork was amazing.

The rest of the room was covered in framed posters of my favorite bands. There was a small fridge under a side table by my bed, and on that side table was a picture of Mom, Lilly, and me when we went on vacation to Disney World the year prior.

Another addition to my little side table—which must have been a gift from Father Jim—a leather-bound copy of The Holy Bible. Even though I had no intentions of reading it, I was touched he went to the trouble of getting me such a nice gift.

Speechless, all I could do was sit with my mouth hanging wide open. The room looked like it had been created by one of those home makeover shows. Honestly, I hadn't even thought of where I would sleep once I got home.

Of course, I loved my old room; it had been the only room I had ever known, but it was upstairs. I had never thought of how trying it would be to get to my room. I suppose it was tainted from the hanging anyway; it was best I had a new room. A new start.

My eyes filled with tears as I tried to put into words how thankful I was, but words failed me. This new room was amazing. If I had friends, they would've been envious of my new digs.

Everyone piled into the room and gave me a hug good-bye. Many of them shared how thankful they were to have met me. *Me? They were thankful to have met me?* I was baffled. The last several months had been a nightmare, and I had verbally abused many of these people.

I couldn't believe that even though I had thrown tantrums and caused them grief, they still cared for me. Without hesitation, I flung my arms open wide for each one of them so I could hug them all. By the time we pulled away from our group hug, we were a sniffling, crying mess.

That night I undressed and maneuvered myself into bed all by myself. It was a great accomplishment for me and the perfect end to my day. The fact that getting ready for bed was made easier by all my new friends from the hospital didn't escape me. The fact that I wouldn't have needed their help to begin with if I hadn't taken life into my own hands didn't escape me either.

As I lay in bed that night, I thought about what life had been like before I made the attempt to end my life, and I also thought of how much it had changed since then. I honestly didn't know if I was happier then or now and that made me sad, but I had to quit living in the past and push on.

My eyes shifted to my side table, and Father Jim's gift caught my eye. For some reason, I felt the need to pick the Bible up. I held it close to my chest and smelled the leather binding. In my heart I felt I owed it to Father Jim to at least try and follow his advice, but first I had something else I needed to do. So, I climbed back out of bed, into my chair, found my bag from the hospital, and dug out the letter Father Jim had given me in the hospital.

Chapter Eleven

Dear Jackson,

I hope this letter will help you understand we all go through struggles. Every single person I've encountered in this world has struggled at some point in their life. The rich can't have enough, the poor need more, children lose parents, parents lose children ...the list goes on and on. But here's what I've learned from my experiences in this world: It's all how you walk away from those situations that matters the most. You of all people should understand life is fragile and it can change in a second.

We can't always help what happens to us in this world but we can help what happens to us in the next. If you take anything away from what I say to you believe this, in this world you find comfort because your mind cannot conceptualize how amazing the next one will be. Trust me, Jesus is preparing a place for you.

About fifty years ago, I was about your age and I didn't think about how short life could be. I was a carefree young man who lived for adventure and was always on the lookout for something fun and exciting. Back in my day, we didn't have video games and fancy phones at our disposal; we had to make our fun. My family lived on a huge farm miles away from town. Most of my fun was exploring the land.

Most of the time, I chose to wander on my own, but every now and then I would take my kid sister with me to get her out of the house. Her name was Julie, and she was much like your sister Lilly. I loved her dearly; she was such a sweet little thing.

One day, I decided to take Julie out with me to the woods. We were on the hunt for adventure. Julie and I had traveled about an hour away from our home when we came upon a cave.

74

It was just the thing we had been searching for! I ventured in first and had gone only about 25 feet into the cave when I heard my sister cry out. I turned around, but she was gone. A large hole had opened up and swallowed her straight into the ground. I rushed over to see how far she had fallen, but I had a hard time judging how far down the hole went. I called out to her, but she didn't answer back.

As fast as I could, I ran all the way home and got help but by the time we came back to get her, she was already gone. The injuries from her fall were too severe. Her limp form being lifted from the hole is something that haunts my dreams to this day.

For years I blamed God. Yes, I believed in Him even then, but I put full blame on Him and then on myself. I went through a vicious cycle of anger and guilt. There was a rage inside of me I couldn't contain. That's when I got into drinking and drugs.

All of my wholesome friends tried to be there for me, but I shut them out. Instead, I hung out with the wrong crowd and got myself into more trouble than I would like to admit. I would like to say I got smart and changed my ways before anything terrible happened but that wasn't so. My drinking problem became so incredibly bad, I rarely knew where I was or what I was doing. One day, I made the decision to drink and drive. That day my old life ended.

The details are ugly and I still have a hard time thinking of them, but essentially I wrapped my car around a tree and was in a coma for six months. When I came back to, my eyes were opened for the first time by a preacher from a local church. He showed me God loved me no matter what, and He would forgive me. I only had to ask Him into my heart. He also taught me how to forgive myself while learning to let the anger and hate that consumed me go. Over time, I was able to let go of my guilt, but it was hard to do...the hardest thing I've ever done in fact. Jackson, I pray you'll have an easier time with this than I did.

The reason I'm telling you this now is because I was in a place where I was self-destructive and had no faith. Anger and hate filled my heart, and I let it dictate how I lived my life. And the worst part of it was, I destroyed everyone around me with my hate. I almost single-handedly destroyed my family while taking myself down a bad path. If it wasn't for God turning the bad into something good, I would've never survived in this world.

Because of what I went through and because of the kindness of that preacher who never gave up on me, I'm now able to be the person I am today. And that's how I've come to serve the Lord in ministry, trying to help young men and women who are broken because of the circumstances they find themselves in. My servitude to the Lord is to do all I can to show God I love Him. He transformed me from a hopeless sinner who was on a path to destruction to a man on fire for the Lord; He can do the same for you.

On the back of this letter, I've written down some passages for you to read out of the Bible. These passages cover the life and death of Jesus Christ our Savior. You must know Christ loves you so much He died to save you from all of your sins no matter how big or small. There's nothing—and I mean nothing—you can do to keep Him from forgiving you or loving you. Please give Christ a chance. He will help you through the tough times and He will help you see His light which will be the light of your life.

Love in Christ,
Father Jim Byers

Father Jim's letter was hard to read. The pain he carried with him must've been terrible. If I'd been in his situation, I don't know if I could've lived through it. Lilly meant the world to me, and if I lost her, I'd die inside. Yet, somehow Father Jim found peace in knowing God. That blew my mind, and I was tempted to read the Bible to see if maybe, just maybe, there were answers in there for me too.

But I wasn't ready, not yet. The day had been eventful and I was worn out. I decided my best course of action was to go to sleep. If I felt the same way in the morning, I would dive right into the Bible and have a look for myself.

For once sleep came quickly, but it was a restless sleep. Dreams of a horrific accident weaved their way into my slumber. There was a young man; his car hit a tree. The tree was laid over the hood of the car, and the windshield had been completely shattered. The young man was stuck in his vehicle. He was crying for help, but no one was close by. He pleaded for someone, anyone, to help. He cried for God and he cursed him, and he cried out the name of a young girl who had been dead for several years— his sister, Julie.

My heart broke for the broken young man. I wanted to call out or go comfort him, but I was unable to move. I tried to call out but had no voice. All I could do was stand there and watch. Out of the corner of my eye something rustled. I squinted in the darkness, looking to see what was there.

There was a man in the clearing not far from where I stood. He too watched the young man. Tears streamed down His face and He did nothing to stop them. Our eyes met, I took in a sharp breath. It was Him: the man from my garden dream, his eyes filled with hurt and pain.

I woke up soaked in sweat and tears. For an hour, I lay in my bed thinking about the young man trapped in his own misery. I tried to put the other man out of my mind, I wasn't ready for Him. Not yet. I wondered if I was much different from the young man in the wreck. trapped with nowhere to go, no one to turn to.

Father Jim had told me God could give us signs and talk to us in different ways. I wondered if these intense dreams were His way of reaching out to me. The dreams felt so real, and seeing that man, whom I believed to be Jesus, really shook me up.

He radiated an overwhelming sensation of love, there are no words to describe how amazing being in His presence truly is. The dreams were starting to scare me. I felt lost and didn't know what to do. I lay in my bed thinking about those dreams for a little while longer before I decided to get up for the day.

Getting ready was going to take me a while since everything at home was so different from the hospital. To get out of bed, I had to get my transfer board which I had wedged in between my bed and nightstand when it wasn't in use. Then I shimmied down from my bed to my wheelchair which I had left close to my bed.

At that point, I would roll over to the closet and get clothes for the day. Thankfully, my mom had someone hang the clothing bar lower, so I could reach my things. After that I had to maneuver out of my door which was almost too small to accommodate my chair.

Thank goodness we had wide hallways, but I had a hard time getting into the bathroom due to the narrow doorway. Since I was already in there getting ready anyway, I decided to try and go to the bathroom as well.

I'm not going to go into details here, but things are definitely different in that regard, like really different. Once I brushed my teeth and combed my hair, I went into the living room to see if Mom or Lilly were up yet. They weren't, so I wheeled around the house and thought about how life was going to be from here on out. This was it. I had two choices: either I could lie down and give up, or make the best of what I had. The new me wanted to embrace it and fight for myself for once.

"Jackson? Why are you up so early?" Mom stumbled into the living room half awake.

"Couldn't sleep," I said as I shrugged my shoulders.

"I guess it feels different from the hospital, huh?" She asked. I nodded my head yes. "You have gotten used to their schedule," she said as she put her hand lightly on my shoulder. Then she asked, "You want some pancakes?"

Mom's pancakes would make for a good morning. I looked up at her. "You have no idea how badly I'd like that."

Life didn't seem so bleak with the prospect of mom's pancakes on the horizon. As she started to work her breakfast magic, I wheeled up to the kitchen table and watched her cook. My mouth was watering by the time she got those bad boys done.

While I ate my pancakes, Mom started some bacon and eggs. I was in heaven; the hospital's food was okay but was nowhere close to my mother's cooking. Of course, I had mainly lived on candy bar bribes from the hospital staff during my stay.

The smell of breakfast cooking must have wafted upstairs and woke Lilly. She came downstairs, her favorite teddy bear curled in her arms. She climbed up on a chair beside me. We had a good morning while Lilly entertained us, filling me in on all I had missed while I was away.

It was amazing. I had never realized how much time like this mattered, just good family time. I felt foolish for not realizing what I had before. Had

I been wiser I would've seen how amazing my life really was. Maybe that was the silver lining in my mistake—never again would I take my family for granted.

~*~

Over the next few months, we got into a groove and life grew easier for me. I believe things got better for my family as well. I was really trying to adapt to my new life, although it proved to be more difficult than I had first thought it would be.

Mom wanted to help, but she knew I had to learn to take care of myself on my own. She meant well, but at times her lack of help caused some frustration. Many days, I wanted her to be my nurse, maid, and mommy. But in the end, she wouldn't relent no matter how much guilt or anger I threw her way. Now, I'm grateful she didn't coddle me. Dr. Sanders was right; I needed to become more independent.

In the end, it was my mother's tough love that helped me become more liberated. But, in the beginning, I was constantly frustrated. All those positive feelings I had felt when I first arrived home quickly evaporated into hostility and anger. That was a trend with me for a long time. I would be positive, happy Jackson until life got hard, then I would do a 180 and act like a punk to everyone around.

Woe is me, I constantly thought,

Most of the time, I was even difficult with Dr. Todd. Some days I think she would've liked to strangle the life out of me. Not that she ever told me that, but I could see it on her face. She came to visit me at the house in the beginning, and she had a lot of insight on the day I had hung myself, but I didn't want to hear it.

I was playing games with everyone. Most of the time I knew I was doing it, but I didn't know how to stop. Amazingly enough, no one gave up on me, and they didn't care how crabby I acted. My crabbiness prevented me from doing a lot of things.

My bad mood kept me from reading the passages Father Jim asked me to read. Every time I thought about it, I'd get so mad about something I couldn't do or something I had a hard time doing that I pushed off reading the Bible. After a while I convinced myself, again, that Father Jim was wrong and there was no point wasting my time on a God who didn't exist. However, the events of the following weeks caused me to think much differently.

Chapter Twelve

For about a month, I'd been stuck in the house going through the motions, but not really doing much of anything. It wasn't long before I was back at a point where I was going through an internal struggle. Part of me wanted to be that positive guy I had started to be, and part of me was downright depressed and didn't care about anything. It was a vicious cycle I didn't know how to get out of.

"Jackson, you've got to get out of the house," Mom said wearily. That day, I was in a nasty mood.

"I don't want to," I snapped.

"I don't care what you want to do, at least take a stroll around the block. You'll feel better, I promise."

"No." I crossed my arms across my chest.

"For the love of God, Jackson, you're driving me crazy today." My mother was about to snap. Her face reddened; she was about to blow.

"Fine, I'll go to the end of the street and back," I said in a feeble attempt to be agreeable. The look of relief on my mom's face was like receiving a kick in the tail.

I wheeled myself to the closet and grabbed my jacket. Pulling my hat from the pocket of my jacket, I crammed it on my head. Although the neighbors knew it was me, I felt less exposed if I wore a hat to conceal my face. Not to mention the cool December air would cut right through me if I didn't.

Once I got out it was nice, although cold, and eventually I forgot I was even in my chair. I kept myself locked in the house so much I forgot how beautiful our neighborhood was, even in the winter.

Our neighborhood was quite nice. All the streets were lined with large oak trees and a sprinkling of cherry wood trees that ran down the middle of the road. The houses weren't stacked right on top of one another, either. That day, I took my time while outside and allowed myself to get lost in the world that surrounded me. It was kind of nice to get away from everyone and think. I'm sure mom needed a few minutes alone as well.

As I wheeled back up the street towards our house, I saw my mother running toward me, frantically waving her arms and shouting my name. My heart skipped a beat; something had happened. "Jackson, we need to hurry. It's Father Jim. It's a…a heart attack." She had come up behind me and began pushing me towards the van.

Mom ran Lilly over to the neighbor's house and was back in no time. The thirty minutes it took to get to the hospital were agonizing. For the first time in my life, I really prayed. I prayed that when I got to the hospital, I would see Father Jim alive.

I kept repeating, "God, if you're real, please save my friend. I'll follow you and your word, if you heal Father Jim."

Now I know there was nothing about that prayer that was right, except the fact that I was praying. All I knew was that Father Jim meant a great deal to me, and I couldn't imagine losing him, not yet. If there was a God, I was calling on Him for a miracle.

My prayers must have worked, as we didn't lose Father Jim that day. But we learned he had a long road to recovery, if he even made it through at all. The nurses told us at his age he might never fully regain his strength. His chances at survival would increase each day, but it was going to be a waiting game.

Visiting hours weren't long and since I wasn't family, I was only permitted to see him for thirty minutes in the morning and thirty minutes at night. It was so hard to see Father Jim the way he was. Wires and tubes covered his body. His skin was pale, almost a transparent gray, and he looked half dead. It struck me that my mother experienced something similar with me.

One thing that helped pass the time in between visits to Father Jim was visiting my support group buddies. The hospital Father Jim was at was about an hour drive from the Manchester Spinal Institute. Mom thought I needed to see my support group more often. As usual, she was right.

I wasn't so sure at first, but in the end they did help me a lot. The first meeting I attended since I left the hospital went pretty great actually. Everyone was there, including Jessica, and we had a great meeting. They all were there for me and helped comfort me in my sorrow over Father Jim.

At the end of our first meeting, I wheeled outside and waited for Mom on the sidewalk. Winter was in full swing and there was a serious chill to the air. Mom texted saying she was running a few minutes late, but I decided to stay outside. I heard wheels running over the pavement and thought maybe Craig or Marv was coming back to say bye before I left, but it wasn't them. It was Jessica. *Gulp.*

"Where's your ride?" she asked.

"Oh, Mom? She's running late. She wanted to get her hair done. She doesn't have much time to take care of herself, ya know?" I said looking down at my chair.

"Yeah, I get that. You want some company?" she asked.

"Uh, sure," I responded with a shrug. For once, the girl seemed normal. I didn't know what to expect from her.

"How have you been?" she asked, her cheeks a rosy pink from harsh wind.

"To be honest, it's been pretty hard, trying to adjust to…everything, you know," I said as I looked over at Jessica wondering why she was being so nice.

"Yeah," Jessica said in almost a whisper. "Is Father Jim okay?"

"He's getting stronger, but he has a long recovery ahead," I said.

"He used to visit me when I first went into the hospital. He's pretty cool," Jessica said.

"Yeah." It was all I knew to say. I had never had a conversation with Jessica that didn't involve yelling, name calling, and the violent storm-off of two wheelchair bound people.

"Listen… Jackson," Jessica began awkwardly. "I um…I may have been a little hard on you when we…you know, during support meetings, and I'm sorry."

Turning to look her way, I smiled sadly. "Thanks. Why were you like that anyway?"

"Well, for several reasons, but mostly—I wanted to be mad at someone. You came along and well…I took my anger out on you."

"Kind of defeats the purpose of being in a support group, huh?"

"Oh…yeah, I suppose so, but I was being selfish. I thought the support should be given to me and not the other way around."

"Yeah, well I'm used to that," I said with a sigh. "There must be something about me that makes people want to yell." Jessica smirked but didn't respond.

Jessica and I sat quietly for several minutes. "I didn't know," she said breaking the silence.

"What?" I asked, completely confused.

"About why you…why you hurt yourself. I would've never…" But I didn't let her finish. I gently placed my hand over hers.

"It's okay," I said. "If I'd been stronger I wouldn't be here, but who knows? Maybe there's a greater purpose than what we understand."

Jessica nodded her head and wiped her eyes with the sleeve of her hoodie. I didn't know if she had been crying or if the cool air made her eyes water.

"No…I don't know how you were able to stand it, then I came along and made the situation worse. I mean even my dad…he didn't mean to you know. He was just…stupid…dumb alcohol, am I right? Can we start over?" She asked shifting uncomfortably in her chair.

I hesitated for a moment. "Yeah, I think so," I said. I wasn't sure if we could, but I didn't want to hurt her feelings. There was something about her that drew me in. I couldn't explain it. There was just something—

Then I saw the top of our van pulling into the parking lot. "Well, there's my mom, umm…I'll see you next week?" I asked.

Jessica looked up at me and smiled, our eyes locked on one another. "Yeah, see you," she said as I wheeled myself to Mom's van.

"Who was that?" Mom asked.

"Oh just a girl from support group," I said.

"I haven't seen her before. She sure is pretty."

"Yeah, she's okay I guess," I said avoiding my mother's hawk-eye stare.

"You want to stop by and say goodnight to Father Jim before we head home?" Mom asked.

"Umm, no, can we can head home now? I'm tired," I said. Father Jim would never know I hadn't made it that day. So far, he had slept through all of my visits.

"Sure, we'll come back tomorrow, okay?"

I nodded and laid my head against the window. My mind was whirling, thinking about Jessica and the feel of my hand against hers.

Chapter Thirteen

During Father Jim's recovery, my mother was amazing and allowed me to visit him several times a week. For the first week, all he did was sleep. His recovery was slow, but I could tell each day he grew stronger. With each passing day, I thought about my promise to God. I hadn't held up my end, and guilt began to plague me. The guilt became so overwhelming I caved and read the passages he had marked for me.

I started with John 3:16 and Matthew 19, and then moved on to the book of Romans. I became a sponge and soaked in the information I was being fed. If nothing else, what I read was…interesting.

For two days, I sat in my room and read the Bible and researched the Internet for articles on Jesus, His love, and the miracles He performed. I took time for food and bathroom breaks but that was about it. I don't even think I showered until the morning of the third day. I didn't even go to see Father Jim; I was lost in God's Word. I couldn't wait to talk to Father Jim about what I'd learned. About what my heart was experiencing.

By the time I finally got back to see Father Jim, he was doing much better, and he noticed a difference in me right away. "Jackson, how are you? You look fantastic, son." His eyes shone with love for me. I was touched when I realized how much he cared for me, and I for him.

"Well," I said, suddenly shy. I don't know why but my newfound faith was personal somehow. "I believe I've made a decision."

"Oh?" he said as one of his eyebrows raised in confusion.

"Yes, I read the passages you asked me to. Then I did some of my own research and, well, I believe God is real. But even more, I prayed for you to be healed and God is healing you!"

"Thank you, Jackson. I appreciate your prayers," Father Jim said, his face growing serious. "But even if God chose to take me to paradise with Him, that would've been okay with me too," he added.

His words shocked me. However, if paradise was anything like the place I had visited in my "garden dream" (minus the tar pit and pillar of smoke), then I could understand not minding to leave this world behind.

"You want to die?" I asked. The fact I had attempted to end my life a few months ago didn't dawn on me as I talked with Father Jim.

"Not exactly, but if God chooses to take me home, then I'm ready. For years, I've done what I feel He's asked me to do and, to be honest with you, Heaven is going to be so wonderful I don't expect to miss this world much."

His words made sense, but at the same time it was a pretty scary concept. I mean, to go to Heaven should be okay, but there is a whole "unknown" element to it all.

"Can I share something with you, Father Jim?" I asked. Suddenly, I felt the need to share my secret.

"Of course," he replied.

So I shared with Father Jim what my life had been like before I hung myself, the day I had hung myself, and even my garden dream. He listened attentively until I was done. "Do you think I'm crazy or do you think it was a dream?" I asked as I finished my tale.

Father Jim took so long answering me, I almost thought maybe he did think I was nuts. But finally he replied, "Jackson, our Lord works in mysterious ways, and I think He knew you would need a little push. There are thousands of accounts where God has reached out to others in many different ways," he told me.

"You know, you really should do some research on it and decide for yourself. Ezekiel is a good place to start, although some of what he says can be confusing at first. With a little research I believe you'll be enlightened in how God works when it comes to…dreams and visions. Me personally? I feel God wants you to forgive your aggressors and he showed you in a way that you would understand—through your perfect garden."

"Jackson, do you believe Jesus is your Savior?" Father Jim's face grew serious.

"Yes, Father Jim, I think I do." Just saying the words aloud filled my heart with joy.

"Do you mind if we pray, Jackson?" he asked.

I shook my head no, I didn't mind at all. As a matter of fact, I wanted to really listen to someone pray so I would know how to do it for myself.

For several minutes, Father Jim and I prayed. Actually, he prayed and I listened. He asked for the Lord to be with me and use me for His will. And I prayed, in my head, God would come into my heart and show me how to be more like Christ.

There I was in the middle of a hospital room with a very sick man accepting the salvation Christ provided me. Looking back now, the scene was touching. But even more than that, my heart was touched by the Holy Spirit, and I was forever changed—although I still had a lot of work to do in my life (Spoiler alert: I *still* do).

Father Jim, after much struggling and shifting to get out of bed, hugged me as I cried tears of joy. I don't think I had ever cried from happiness before. That is a day I'll never forget—the day I became saved, and I've never looked back.

Chapter Fourteen

On the way home from the hospital, I decided to talk to Mom about my decision and see how she felt about us as a family making some much needed changes in our lives. "How do you feel about going to church?" I asked, looking at her as she watched the road intently.

"Hmm, well…I…think that would be okay if it's what you want to do," she said. I noticed her white-knuckle grip on the steering wheel.

"Well, Mom, I've been fighting it for a while now, but I really do think we all need to change our lives. You know, there's a big difference between being a good person and being a Christian," I said.

Mom nodded her head and smiled, and she relaxed her grip a little. "Yes, I suppose there is."

"What do you think about religion and—stuff?" I asked. Learning to overcome my vulnerability was difficult when it came to discussing my faith. It was all so new and a bit personal.

"Well, it's complicated, Jackson. I guess you could say I believe in God, but we had a falling out." She looked unsure as to whether she wanted to talk to me about the subject at all.

"Well, maybe it's time for you to make up," I said. I didn't want to press her on what she and God may not have agreed on, but I would've bet money it had to do with my dad leaving. "How about we find a church and see how we like it?" I asked. "If you don't feel comfortable, maybe Lilly and I can go…like on a bus or something."

"You know what…let's try it and see what happens," Mom said. She reached over and gave my hand a little squeeze.

It made me feel good to see she was open to the idea. It would've been difficult for me if she didn't want to try.

~*~

Once we were back at home, Mom disappeared for a while. I went to my room to research Ezekiel. Father Jim was right—it was confusing, but once I did some research I started to understand my garden dream may not have been just a dream. More than ever I felt the need to find a church and seek the answers I needed about God and how He operates. I needed to talk to my mother.

I found her sitting on the back porch staring into the horizon. "Mom? You okay?"

"Oh yes, of course. I was just thinking." She paused for a minute. "I never thought my kids would teach me more than I've taught them, is all."

"What do you mean?" I asked.

"I had no idea what you went though. I still don't, not really. I mean I know what you say happened but I can't even imagine feeling so isolated and alone."

"Mom, it's ok…"

"No, it's not okay. It will be, I think—but not yet. You see, I've been foolish. I had faith in God but when your dad…when he left…I blamed God. I…hated Him, not for what your dad did to me, but for the pain that you and Lilly would go through. And then I hated Him more when I sat at your bedside hoping you would survive. Wondering how someone with such a beautiful heart had to suffer so terribly."

"Ma…"

"It's fine really," she looked over at me with tear-filled eyes. "You see, this very afternoon a very brave young man witnessed to me in a small yet mighty way. And for the first time, I began to question my decision of walking away from God. If you went through such a terrible ordeal and are still willing to seek Him then maybe I should give it a whirl as well."

"You mean *me*?" I asked dubiously.

"Yes, love, you. Don't underestimate how powerful your testimony can be, Jackson. Because of what you shared with me…now I think it may be time for our family to invite God into our lives."

I looked over to my little garden. It had withered away for the winter, but it would flourish again soon. I smiled over at my mother. "Yeah, it's definitely time."

As it turned out, that following Sunday we found the right church for our family. It was a large older building with stained glass everywhere. It was a beautiful place to look at, but what was inside was truly amazing. The people were true treasures. They welcomed us immediately and made us feel like family. They embraced us as if we were long lost family members. In a way, I guess we were.

Right away we were taken to Sunday school classes and given information about activities available to Lilly, which was a bonus for our family. Also, there was a singles class for Mom to go to. I knew she would find good support there.

The youth group impressed me the most. Everyone was super cool and really made me feel welcome. No one made me feel weird for being in a chair at all. To be honest, the adults stared more than kids my age did. The kids in the youth group wanted to play with my chair and didn't shun me.

Mom and I had decided it would be best if we found a church a little farther away from our home and school so I would be less likely to run into my old bullies. It was a good idea and we didn't run into my old bullies; however, I did run into Brittney Wagner.

The fact that Brittney and I would attend the same church wasn't revealed to me for a few weeks, as she and her family were away for Christmas break. When she walked into the youth room on my third Sunday there, all the air in my lungs rushed out in one quick breath. She spotted me instantly and froze in the doorway. The distress in her eyes made me feel bad for her. She turned back like she was ready to run back the way she had come. Yet, for the first time since my ordeal, I was relieved to find I wasn't angry when I saw her.

Anger had been my typical response when we happened to bump into each other around town, which was only a handful of times since my "incident". I was relieved to find the anger had gone; however, I wasn't really ready to talk to her.

To keep the peace and to ensure I gave off a positive vibe I gave her a friendly nod to acknowledge she was there. She gave me a small smile and nodded back. She then quickly hurried over to a group of girls who were part of the youth group. I hoped she didn't say anything that would make my new friends think differently about me. To this day I don't think she ever did.

For a few weeks Brittney left me alone, but that was about as long as she was willing to wait to talk to me. Then out of the blue one Sunday morning before class started, she approached me.

"Hi," she said, twirling her hair around her finger looking anywhere but at me.

"Hey, how's it going?" I asked politely.

"Um…good…I was thinking…maybe me and you should talk…ya know, work through everything that's happened since…" Brittney was really having a hard time spitting out what she was wanting to say. I knew what she was getting at, so I saved her the struggle.

"Yeah, we probably should," I said running my hands through my hair. "How about today after church? You can come over for lunch. I'm sure my mom won't mind," I said. "If, of course, it's okay with you and your parents."

"Um…I think that'd be okay…if you're sure," Brittney sputtered.

I shrugged my shoulders. "It's fine with me," I said.

"Okay, I'll meet you after church then." Brittney looked as if she was partly relieved and partly terrified. It wasn't a good look for her. Hopefully after today we could both move past what had happened.

"Sure…see ya then." Now, I was starting to feel awkward. I really hoped Brittney and I could work through our differences. All I could do was pray about it, which is what I did all through the church service.

~*~

"Wow, your mom's a great cook," Brittney said an hour and a half later as she slid her plate away from her.

"You have no idea," I said as I cleared my own plate. I'd put a few extra pounds on since I had been home from the hospital. In my case it was a good thing, as I had lost a lot the first several months after my stay.

Mom was an excellent cook and her lasagna made from scratch was the best she ever made. I ate two large pieces of the cheesy goodness.

Mom was close by and she beamed under the praise. I always wondered why she never went into cooking professionally. I asked her once and she said she was afraid if she cooked all day every day, she may not enjoy it as much when she got home. That made sense to me, so I didn't bug her about it. I didn't care if she cooked well for others as long as she cooked for me. Either way, mom's cooking was a great way to break the ice for Brittney and me.

"Well, Jackson, Lilly and I are going outside. I need some air. You and Brittney help yourselves to some apple pie whenever you're ready," Mom said as she cleared our plates away and set down an apple pie chock-full of sweet delicious apple slices.

"Thanks, Mom," I said.

"Yes, thank you Mrs. Liddle," Brittney said kindly.

By now my mom knew what had gone down between Brittney and me. When we started going to church, I had revealed to Mom what I had gone through at school and with Brittney, so she knew Brittney and I needed to talk. She wasn't impressed with how Brittney had left me hanging at the lowest point in my life, but since Christ had touched her heart, she had been trying to be more forgiving.

Mom smiled warmly at both of us and then she and Lilly left us alone to chisel away at the stone that had wedged itself between our friendship.

Talking was difficult for us at first, but we were taking it as it came. My biggest obstacle was forgiving Brittney. Now I realized I had placed too much blame on her back then and not nearly enough on myself.

"It's good to see you at church, Jackson," Brittney started when we were alone. "Since that day at school…I've prayed and prayed for you." She looked down at her hands. "I kind of feel like God wanted us to meet up and work our differences out."

I knew what she meant. I felt the same way, after the initial shock of knowing we were going to be a part of the same church family wore off. We both knew a divine intervention brought us back together, I mean, what were the odds we'd end up going to the same church after everything we'd been through? I knew God was at work. It felt good knowing He was in on every aspect of my life. That's how I knew everything would be okay because He was always there.

"Yeah, I think so, too," I replied. "Listen, I'm really trying to change my life, but when it comes to you I'm having a hard time. Honestly, I think I've been able to forgive Brett, but for some reason I was more hurt by you than anyone."

"Yeah, I would've felt the same way if it were me. Jackson, please know I'm so sorry. When everything happened that day, I didn't know what to do. I panicked and left." She held her hands palms up as if she was as confused as I was. "I've thought about that day so many times and I had no good reason for leaving you there. Your face is all I see when I go to bed at night."

"I want to make an effort to rebuild our friendship, but it is going to take time," I said slowly.

I was definitely scared to throw myself back out there to potentially get hurt again, but one thing my relationship with Christ had shown me was I could do all things with God on my side. "You know…" I let out a huge breath. "I do blame myself a little." That was the first time I admitted that out loud, maybe even to myself.

"Why do you blame yourself?" Brittney's eyes opened wide in confusion. "You didn't do anything to deserve that kind of treatment."

"Maybe not, but I could've told someone who would help. Maybe I could've stood up for myself sooner. If I hadn't let it go on for so long, maybe the bullying wouldn't have been so bad."

Saying it out loud hurt, but I had to take ownership in my part of it all. "My life's been changed forever; there's no reason in the world I should've made an attempt to take my own life. Things got out of hand." That was a decision I was going to have to live with for the rest of my life, but with God's help, I would be able to forgive myself. I wasn't there yet but one day—

"I wished you hadn't done it either, Jackson, but I know God can take the bad and turn it into something good. Don't forget that." Brittney's words were soaked with passion when she spoke of God. I smiled, hoping one day my faith would be that strong. Her words inspired me, and gave me hope. Maybe she was right. Maybe God could turn my situation into something good.

"Do you really think He can forgive me?" It was something I was concerned about, if God could really forgive someone like me.

"He's just waiting for you to ask, Jesus already paid the price for all you've done and all you will do. Open your heart to Him and have a true conversation. Let Him know how you feel and what your heart desires. He'll hear you, but you have to mean it. Give it all to Him and don't let it linger in your heart." I needed to hear those words so badly.

My heart filled with hope, yet there was still something bothering me— something I hadn't even acknowledged in my prayers.

"Wow, that's deep," I said.

Brittney laughed, slightly embarrassed. "It's what Pastor Robins told me when he counseled me after your...when you were in the hospital."

"I didn't know—" I started.

"There was this guilt, you know. I should've been there for you...I should've had your back." She confessed.

"We didn't...you had no way of knowing what I was going to do." *Really, who did?* I wasn't even sure I knew what I was doing.

"No, I didn't, but I had to learn to forgive myself and ask God to forgive me for my part as well. It was difficult and sometimes that overwhelming feeling of failure overtakes me." *Guilt is a heavy thing to contend with*, I thought.

"Yeah, I know what you mean. It still gets me too," I said.

"God can forgive us everything," she said looking down at the table. Things were getting very serious for both of us.

"But...I went outside of God's plan? How can He forgive that?" There might have been a slight whine to my voice.

"But did you succeed?" She asked.

"No...Wait, what do you mean?"

"Do you think you ruined God's plan for your life? I doubt it. Maybe your story is different than it could've been, but God knows you. He has a plan for you and you went off course, but I think He can still use you for His glory." She placed her hand over mine and looked intently at me. "We're all human, Jackson, and we make mistakes. Sometimes, we don't even realize what we do is wrong until it's too late, but nothing is too late for God."

Her closeness unnerved me. I was at a loss for words, but she was probably right. God didn't expect us to be perfect; He wanted us to spread His love and live by His words. And if we slipped up, then He wanted us to ask for forgiveness and try hard not to sin in that way again. I wondered why that's so hard to do—to admit we're wrong and ask to be forgiven. And even harder to believe we are truly forgiven.

After a few tense moments, Brittney and I changed the subject and the conversation moved to my condition and what had happened while I was a patient in the hospital. I told her about everything except my dream. I didn't want her to think I was nuts. Father Jim understood, but I wasn't sure Brittney would, so I stuck to that which happened on this side of creation.

For the most part, Brittney sat and listened to me as I talked. It felt really good to have someone to talk to. Dr. Todd was amazing, but she was paid to listen to me. And I loved Father Jim, but it wasn't the same as someone my own age. We (mostly me) talked for over two hours before Mom came in to offer Brittney a ride home. It sounds crazy, but I almost hated to see her go. However, I had a feeling we would have many more days together to rebuild our friendship. I no longer had a burning love for Brittney, but I did want to be her friend. I was contemplating that when Brittney's voice interrupted my thoughts.

"Oh wait, I had something else to tell you, I almost forgot!" she exclaimed. "Mrs. Jennie, the Children's Ministry Leader at our church, is also involved in the Anti-Bullying Association, she wanted to know if you'd be willing to talk with kids who—who may be in similar situations as you were?"

I hesitated, then said, "Well…we'll see. I don't know if I'm ready to talk about it yet. When does she need an answer?" I asked.

"She didn't really say, but you don't have to do it, you know. I thought I'd pass the information to you, but if you need more time…" I could tell she was scared I was going to get angry, but I wasn't, truly.

"I'll think about it, but how did she know what had happened to me?" I asked more curious than upset.

I knew it was only a matter of time before word got out to my church family. I had hoped it would have taken a little longer.

"I really don't know." She shrugged her shoulders. "I never told anyone."

My mom, standing in the doorway, sheepishly 'fessed up. "It was me. Sorry, I shouldn't have said anything, but Mrs. Jennie really is a huge advocate for bullied kids and I found myself needing someone to talk to."

Her cheeks grew a little red and she looked slightly ashamed, but I realized I wasn't the only one who had suffered a trauma, and Mom needed people to talk to as well.

"It's okay, Mom, no biggie." I couldn't expect Mom to not talk about what she'd been through. Really, I was surprised no one had asked me what happened yet.

"Okay, well, I am going to run Brittney home. You want to go?" Mom asked.

"Nah, I've got...some stuff to do around here." Mom gave me a weird look, but she didn't say anything. I mean, there was nothing around the house for me to do, but I wanted to be alone and think about all that had developed since I had left church that morning. It had been a big day.

Once Mom, Brittney, and Lilly left I logged onto my computer and looked up the Anti-Bullying Association. I was amazed to see the statistics on how many kids just like me were being bullied every day. For hours, I was sucked into stories of kids who were beaten and tortured, and many kids like me who tried to take their own lives.

Sadly, most of them succeeded. As a matter of fact, I didn't see any cases where a kid hung themselves and lived to tell about it. Without a doubt, I knew I was fortunate God gave me a second chance, but I was sickened seeing how many kids ended up dead and it made me wonder why I was so blessed.

As I was sucked into the computer, reading story after story and statistic after statistic, my cell phone rang. It was Jessica. We'd been talking a lot since we made peace that day in the parking lot. It felt good to talk to Jess as I told her about my day with Brittney and all the research I'd been doing that afternoon.

"Some of these kids were eight, nine, ten years old. They had their whole lives to live," I said, my voice cracking.

The videos of the surviving family members grieving over their loved ones were the worst. I realized how much I had grown and changed since the day I had hung myself. My deepest regret was that I wished I had accepted Christ earlier. I now had a yearning deep inside me that wanted to spread His love so I could save kids like me from the pain and heartache which could lead to them taking their lives.

"Jackson, maybe you can help kids who are in the same situation, before it's too late." It's creepy how Jessica reads my mind. It happens all the time.

"Yeah, a lady at church wants me to be an advocate for the Anti-Bullying Association, but I don't know..." I said.

"You chicken," Jessica fired. "What are you scared of? The worst has already happened."

Oh Jessica, she never has any problem telling me how she feels, and usually she's right.

"Man, you are tough. You know that?" I said with a smile. She was right. I needed to help, no matter how hard it was going to be.

"Yeah, that's why you need me in your life," she teased. I wanted to say something then about how I needed her in my life for more, but I didn't. For a while now, I was thinking maybe I needed Jessica as more than a friend, but past experience held me back. I had plenty of time to find the right girl. I believed God would put her in my path and if that girl happened to be Jessica, then even better.

"Yeah, I needed a grumpy, pushy, beauty queen in my life to keep me straight. However would I live without you?" I kidded her back.

"Shut your face," Jessica said, laughing.

Her laugh made me smile. There wasn't a day that went by that Jessica didn't make me smile. She was amazing. We talked for a few more minutes, and then said our good-byes for the evening.

Before I went to bed that night, I prayed long and hard about what I should do about speaking to bullied children. The mere thought of telling my story to strangers caused me to feel nauseous, but I wanted to put it in God's hands. I don't remember having any particularly weird experience to indicate I should have or shouldn't have agreed to help Mrs. Jennie. However, when I woke up I was determined to do what God had laid on my heart.

I got Mrs. Jennie's phone number from Mom and agreed to help other kids like me. The next call I made was to my youth director, Mr. James, and asked if I could share my story with our youth group. He agreed to let me talk, but since my story involved a suicide attempt, he had to talk with the parents of the youth first.

I understood that. I didn't want others to feel like my decision to end my life was okay. In fact, I wanted to share with them that my deepest regret was hurting myself. My final call was to Father Jim. I needed him to help me with my story and to pray for me. In my heart, I knew he would understand my anxiety about sharing something so private.

In the end everything worked out. All the youths' parents agreed to let me share my story. To save her any pain or torment, I didn't mention Brittney. I changed her name to protect her. This was good, as my new friends instantly took a disliking to "Sarah," aka Brittney. All the youth seemed to be really supportive in what I went through, and it brought me closer to the group.

Life finally started to turn out okay for me from that point on. Life in a "chair" was still tough, but for the first time in years I had real friends, and those friends wanted to become a part of the Anti-Bullying Association as well. They wanted to take a stand and put an end to bullying. Some of my new friends admitted that they'd been bullies themselves and until they'd met me they didn't realize how terribly words and actions could impact another person's life.

On weekdays, some of the guys from my youth group would come over and hang out and we would play video games. Every now and then, I would have sleepovers and we'd play basketball, which I might add I got really good at after some practice. My new friends made me realize that life was just starting and there was so much more I had to offer. I wish I had met them a year prior.

Aside from my newfound friendships, I was growing a relationship with God which was amazing. My love for Him sparked a fire in me to be an advocate for the Anti-Bullying Association. In the years that followed, I visited many different schools and shared with other kids and their parents what I had been through.

Eventually, I went on to speak all over the United States. The best part was that I was able to witness to others about Christ. God took my terrible situation and turned it into a way to spread His love. Unfortunately, there was one more thing from my past I had to deal with, and he ended up coming to me.

Chapter Fifteen

It was through my brokenness that I found you.
The brightness I sought from this world dulled,
allowing me to be filled with eternal glory.
Now I know, now I know, that you love me.
And now I know, you complete me.

After I'd been out of the hospital for around eight months, my life once again took a strange turn. It was around five o'clock on a Friday afternoon, Mom, Lilly, and I had just arrived home from a day of appointments. Fridays were crazy. I saw Dr. Todd in the mornings and a physical therapist in the afternoon.

That particular Friday we had to go to the Manchester Spinal Institute for a follow-up and a support group meeting. My friends there were willing to change their days and times around so I could be there with them. Thus, it had been a long day and I was ready to lie down and relax for a while before supper. However, that evening I wasn't going to relax until much later.

The doorbell rang as I wheeled myself to my bedroom for a nap before dinner. Mom yelled for me to get the door while she deboned a chicken. So I busted a U-turn in the middle of the living room. To my surprise, Brett Watters' hulking form stood before me. He had always been intimidating to me but sitting three feet closer to the ground caused me great discomfort.

For a moment, I thought he was there to follow through with his threat to make my life miserable, but after taking a good look at him, I realized that wasn't going to happen. As a matter of fact, Brett looked like he was afraid *I* was going to hurt *him*. His face was pale and his hands shook slightly. It appeared as if he was trying to speak but no words came out.

Mom strolled up behind me to see who had come for an unannounced visit. Since neither Brett nor myself was making any progress in the talking department, Mom interceded. "Who do we have here?" She asked, drying her hands on an old dish towel.

"Uhhhh," I started but Brett cut me off.

"Hello…Mrs.…Mrs.…Liddle. My name is Brett Watters and I would like to speak with Jackson." Brett sputtered, wringing his hands.

My head jerked towards my mother to see how she received Brett's presence in our home. By this time, she had heard all about him, and I knew her reaction wouldn't be good. She was able to put her feelings aside where Brittney was concerned, but Brett was a different story.

The first time I had told mom about Brett and all that had happened, she was ready to have his head. It was all I could do to stop her from finding where he lived and getting a hold of him. Based on the look on her face now, her feelings hadn't changed much since then. Her eyes widened and her nostrils flared like a raging bull.

"Mom, it's…it's okay. I think Brett and I should talk." I spoke firmly so Mom knew I meant what I said.

"Hmph, okay, but don't be long. Dinner will be ready soon. And you better watch how you talk to my son, you understand me?" With a menacing look at Brett, my mom turned on her heels and went back into the kitchen.

"Man, she's scary," Brett mumbled.

"You have no idea," I shot back before thinking. We both kind of chuckled for a second until the conversation turned serious again.

"Um, Brett, why are you here?" I wasn't going to beat around the bush with this guy. I was no longer scared of what he might do. I mean, I was, but my mom was around and I felt a little braver with her so close.

"Listen, this is hard for me, but…can we sit and talk for a few minutes?" Brett was looking everywhere but at me.

"Sure, I'm already sitting," I said, with a twinge of sarcasm. I had to remind myself not to be that way.

At that cheap shot Brett's cheeks turned red. "Yeah, I guess you are," he said.

His eyes examined the chair and I could feel his discomfort intensify. Quickly, he averted his eyes to the rosebushes that climbed the lattice alongside the house. He stood there for a while, rubbing the back of his neck with his large hands.

My entire stay in the hospital I wanted nothing more than to see Brett pay for what he did to me. However, as he stood before me, his shoulders hunched in surrender, I no longer felt that way. "Okay, Brett, have a seat and let's talk, but I go first." I was serious, and Brett respected that.

"Okay, fine," he said with a defeated shrug. I yelled to Mom I would be outside, and she yelled back to be on time for dinner or else. She was taking the anger she felt for Brett's intrusion out on a poor chicken that was supposed to be dinner.

Once settled on the porch, I started with how Brett had made me feel for all of those years, but I made a point to talk mostly about the day I hung myself—not to hurt him but so he could understand what his actions had done. I also wanted to tell him no matter how bad the world became, God had a plan for me and He was going to use me for His plan.

For thirty minutes straight, I talked and witnessed about what God had done in my life. To his credit, Brett listened and didn't say a word. Once I ran out of steam, I gave Brett a chance to speak.

He was nervous, but listening to me talk had loosened him up a bit. "Jackson, I want to start by saying I'm sorry man, I was evil and cruel to you. There was no reason for me to put you through what I did. You didn't deserve that." From what I could tell he seemed sincere.

"But why me?" I asked, really needing to know the answer to that question. It was something I had asked myself over and over, and I felt I deserved an answer.

Brett shrugged. "You were always happy and I wasn't. I was going through a rough time and you were an easy target, and I guess—" he sighed, "because you let me."

His words were so matter of fact it shocked me. I expected him to say he didn't know why or maybe he didn't realize how bad his life had gotten. His raw honesty took me aback, but I respected his answer, even if I didn't like it.

"What could you possibly have gone through that would allow you to torture me for all those years?" I was dumbfounded.

"My dad," Brett started, then he stopped. "He…uh…he passed away." Brett finished with a shrug.

"I am sorry. When?" I could understand losing a parent would cause some bad emotions, but that didn't explain why I suffered the brunt of Brett's distress.

"About three months ago," Brett said, but his eyes didn't show sadness. Looking at Brett, he seemed happier. His whole disposition was completely different; he almost looked like a new person. There was a kindness and understanding to his eyes, but there was a deep sadness there as well.

"But…you haven't seen me since then." I wasn't trying to pry but I was seriously confused on how his dad's death had anything to do with me.

"My dad was an alcoholic; he beat me and my kid brother. Sometimes he would get a hold of my mom. There was nothing anyone could do to stop him. Mom tried to run and hide but he would always find us. We tried having him thrown in jail, but the beatings become much worse when he got out so we learned to just accept it. My little brother...he...he's scarred for life, man." Brett clenched his jaw.

"Look Brett, if you're not ready to talk about this, let me know and we can do this another time," I started, but Brett was adamant about finishing what he had come to do.

"No, I should've come a long time ago...as soon as all this mess started. But...see, my life was a mess when I had started picking at you and it stayed that way until recently. The school called my dad and threatened to press charges. I wasn't able to go back to school for a week after the beating he gave me." A heavy rush of air poured from Brett's flared nostrils, he paused and looked up at me, his brown eyes reflecting guilt, pain, and remorse.

"Lately, I have learned what peace is, and most of the anger kind of melted away when my dad died. That's when I realized, you didn't deserve how I treated you. I needed to see if you could forgive me, or at the very least I needed you to know it wasn't your fault." Brett had been looking down at his calloused hands, but now he looked up at me and his eyes searched mine. I knew God wanted me to make peace with him.

"Yes, Brett, I do forgive you. In fact, I forgave you months ago, around the time I asked God into my heart." I was serious about that. I had forgiven him, but it was hard to forget the pain he had put me through.

There were still days when I had flashbacks of everything he'd done and it felt like someone took a sledge hammer to my gut filling me with anger and embarrassment, but I knew it was an enemy attack. There's no way I'd allow myself to be pulled back down into the darkness that had almost consumed me, not with God on my side.

Brett let out a huge sigh. "Thank you." He shook his head in disbelief that I could so easily forgive him.

It was quite moving, really. If God hadn't changed me so drastically several months ago, I wouldn't have been so compassionate towards Brett now.

Mom was peering through the living room window beckoning me to come in for dinner. I don't think she realized that she was still clutching the butcher knife in her hand...or maybe she did. Either way Brett shot to his feet, ready to dive off the deck if Mom came to the front door. "Brett, I have to go. Thank you for apologizing. It means a lot, really," I said quickly, then I extended my hand. "For years I thought there was something wrong with me. Knowing that there was more to all this has given me a little peace."

"No, the only thing wrong with you is you let me get away with it for so long," Brett said as he shook my hand. "Honestly, I don't even think that's a bad trait to have, it shows that you have always been a better man than me."

"Sounds like you are on the right track now. It takes a lot to apologize for something like this," I said as I started to wheel my chair back toward my house. "Um, Brett, listen, you didn't make me hang myself, you know? I made that decision on my own so...so don't beat yourself up about that part of it."

"Thanks for saying that, but if not for me you may have never felt that way to start with."

"If you ever need to talk," I started, but I didn't know how to finish what I wanted to tell him. It was crazy, I almost wanted to be his friend.

"Yeah...I got ya, maybe I'll take you up on that," Brett said as he turned and walked away. As he got about halfway down our driveway, he turned to me and said, "You know, I wish we had been friends...you're all right, Liddle."

I smiled at Brett and waved good-bye. It was nice to hear from him, his acceptance meant a lot to me.

Mom was waiting for me as soon as I rolled into the house. "Well, what did he have to say?" She was fired up; her face was still a shade of red which could only be found in a can of paint. The vicious lioness ready to protect her handicapped cub.

"Actually, he apologized," I said. Then I filled her in on the conversation while we ate dinner.

Hearing about what he and his family had endured really opened our eyes. There is always more to a story than what appears on the surface. I wished I'd considered the possibility months earlier that Brett had something going on at home, that maybe the problem was him and not me. Maybe it would've made a difference on how I had handled the situation.

My mother and I both felt bad for Brett. His life must have been so rough he had to make someone else feel as isolated and alone as he did. The bad part was no one knew this was going on in his life. He carried his burden alone, much like I had.

"I guess it goes to show we never know what is going on in someone's life," Mom said, deep in thought.

"Yeah, no kidding," I said, still a little stunned by Brett's revelation. "I would've never thought Brett, of all people..."

"What people put up with will surprise you." Mom looked pointedly at me.

Knowing I had hid a lot from my loved ones as well, I started to turn a little red. Had I not kept secrets from my mother, life would probably be different for me now.

"I know, Mom, but from now on I am going to tell you everything," I said.

"Oh yeah? Well in that case what's up with you and Jessica?" Mom shot back.

"Good-night." I grinned as I quickly wheeled to my room, pretending I didn't hear her question. *Maybe there are still a few things I'm not quite ready to talk about*, I thought, as the sound of mom's laughter followed me to my room.

Chapter Sixteen

That night before bed I stared out my window looking at the stars and thinking about how much life had changed for me over the last year. I went from a physically healthy but mentally abused teen, to a physically broken but spiritually fulfilled young man. In my heart, I wished I had found God before everything had happened. But I was so glad He was there when I was ready to accept Him into my life. As a matter of fact, I had a distinct feeling God had some big plans for me, plans that may not have happened if I hadn't come through my trials and learned how to forgive.

Sleep came swiftly that night, and I found myself dreaming of my special garden. It was as beautiful as I remembered it. This time I took my time exploring and found some of the most amazing places. There was a little cove covered in soft moss and tiny white flowers. The garden was a place you could sit for hours and talk to God. It was almost as if I was closer to Him there.

In my heart I hoped I would always be able to come back to this special place, but I had a feeling this would be my last visit. I was there for a purpose and it wasn't to sightsee. I had to go to the base of the mountain. God wanted me to see the damage created by the smoke and the ground eating tar.

It didn't take long to find the place I was searching for. There were no more tiny fires eating away at the land. The area was still gray and withered, but the thick smoke no longer clung to the air, and upon closer inspection, I observed bright green tufts of grass peeking through the ash.

With dread, I sought out the mini black lake to see if it was still there. I found it, or I found the spot it had occupied months ago. Now, it had all but dried up, and in the middle of where the puddle once lay was a small sapling sprig breaking though the ground.

As I stood looking around me at what was once devastation, I felt hope for what was to come. Over time this pile of dust would return to its former glory. Who knows, this little spot may be stronger for overcoming such devastation. As that thought crossed my mind, I felt the presence of the Lord fill my heart and I said good-bye to my special place, knowing I might not see it again in this life, but I did know I would always carry it with me in my heart.

Epilogue

"Bullying is a serious problem many children face. Every. Single. Day. On any given school day, hundreds of children skip school or feign illness because they're afraid of falling victim to bullies. We lose children to suicide every year—in fact, it is the third leading killer of teens. Our children cannot handle the abuse they endure from their peers. Many of our children feel they have nowhere to turn, and depression overtakes their minds until they can no longer take the sadness that plagues them. Families are devastated due to the loss of their precious loved ones. We have to find a way to spread awareness to everyone so we can stop this behavior in our children."

Mrs. Jennie spoke passionately about the subject she cared so deeply about.

"Most children who attempt suicide are successful and before their family members know there is a problem, it is too late. Today, ladies and gentleman, I want to introduce you to an extraordinary young man who has overcome many different obstacles, and his biggest obstacle was his attempted suicide. Most of his life this young man was bullied, and the bullying became so horrific he attempted suicide, like so many young people do across the nation. Fortunately for all of us here, he survived, and now he shares his story in order to bring awareness to a crisis that's still very much a problem in our society. This young man is the voice for the children we've lost. This young man not only had to overcome his insecurities from being bullied for several years, but he also had to overcome these insecurities as a paraplegic."

Mrs. Jennie turned to look at me. "Jackson Liddle will spend the rest of his life in a wheelchair because he hung himself to end the torment he faced day after day." A shocked silence washed over the audience and many people shifted uncomfortably in their seats.

I was used to their discomfort; however, by the time they went home that night I would make sure they didn't feel sorry for me. They had no reason to, because in the last eight years I'd been blessed beyond measure. Don't get me wrong: life was tough, and sometimes I was bitter, but through it all God blessed me with way more than I deserved.

"Without further ado please welcome Jackson Liddle to the stage." The crowd erupted in applause as I wheeled my chair forward to share my story. For several years I had been giving speeches around the country, yet I still grew nervous every single time.

I cleared my throat and lifted my face in the biggest smile possible. "Thank you so much for being here this evening as I share with you my story. Tonight my presentation will be a little different than what you may be expecting. For one, the presence of God is the most important aspect of my life so you will hear how important He has been to my recovery." My eyes scanned the audience observing how they received this bit of news. In some areas the crowd grew uncomfortable at the mention of God, but this was my calling and I wasn't going to let Him down after all He had sacrificed for me. This particular audience seemed okay with the mention of God, which allowed me to relax a little.

"Also, I cannot tell my story without introducing you to a person who is so important to that part of my life." I turned my head to look over at Brett. His face was a sickly green, this was his first time speaking, but I knew he would do great. "Please give a hand to my bully, Brett Watters."

The room grew silent, then murmurs arose from the audience like a swarm of mad hornets. So I started to clap loudly, and the rest of the audience followed suit but only half-heartedly. It was unnerving to see the looks on many of their faces, but we were there to do what God had asked us to do and there was no going back.

"He...hello, I am Brett Watters, Jackson's bu...bully..."

For the next hour, Brett and I told our stories and how they intertwined. It actually went off well, and there were tears from the audience, from Brett, and from myself. No matter how many times I spoke, it still got to me. Our tale was a shocking series of events, but in the end we came out of it okay—better than okay. I looked up at my best friend as he thanked the audience and then mouthed a special thank you to another special friend of mine and Brett's—his fiancée, the lovely Brittney Wagner.

Life worked out really funny for all of us. Shortly after Brett apologized to me, we started talking every few weeks and built a one-of-a-kind friendship. About a year later he started coming to church with me and from there our friendship bloomed. Brittney and the reformed Brett hit it off and have been inseparable ever since. They are two of my dearest friends, and I am incredibly happy for them.

As for me, God blessed me with an amazing girl who helps keep me strong when I want to give up. Jessica, my support group buddy, became so much more. She's amazing and we plan to get married in the fall once she graduates college. My dearest friend of all, Father Jim, will stand by my side as my best man.

Almost nine years prior I was at my lowest point, so low in fact I had wanted my life to end. Now, however, I look forward to the future and what God has in store for me. Remember, no matter how bleak life may seem, give God a chance. Put your life in His hands and trust that He will guide you to a path of righteousness.

May God's love fill your soul.

ABOUT THE AUTHOR

Rachel was born and raised in Hardin County, Kentucky. She loves spending time learning new things and is an avid hobby collector. Rachel loves spending time with her three beautiful daughters and awesome husband. She adores chocolate and is obsessed with all things Harry Potter. To learn more about Rachel and to connect with her on social media click on the links below.

https://www.facebook.com/RachelRenayLopez
https://www.instagram.com/rachelrenaylopez/
https://twitter.com/rachel_r_lopez
https://rachelrlopez.com/

Other books by Rachel Lopez

The Water Cave: Book One in the Transporter Series
The Cave of Darkness: Book Two in the Transporter Series
A Home for Noel

Coming Soon

The Fire Cave: Book Three of the Transporter Series

Made in the USA
Las Vegas, NV
01 June 2021

23990584R00069